A Body at Book Club

A Myrtle Clover Cozy Mystery, Volume 6

Elizabeth Spann Craig

Published by Elizabeth Spann Craig, 2019.

A BODY AT BOOK CLUB

First edition. August 7, 2019.

Written by Elizabeth Spann Craig.

For the teachers who helped me become the writer I am today.

Chapter One

It was another steamy hot summer afternoon and Myrtle Clover was keeping cool indoors by staying glued to *Tomorrow's Promise,* her favorite soap opera. Her avid viewing of Kayla's daring rescue from a bizarre cult was suddenly and rudely interrupted by a cat's screaming wail and the sound of dogs snapping and growling outside.

"Pasha!" she gasped, struggling to her feet from the padded softness of her recliner and knocking a half-finished crossword puzzle from her lap. Grabbing her cane in one hand and seizing a nearby pitcher of lemonade in the other, she bolted out the front door.

Two large dogs were on her front walk, snapping at and nosing a black, hissing, frightened cat that was trapped between them and fighting to get out. Myrtle bellowed, "Stop!" and flung the lemonade at the animals. The dogs stopped, swinging their heads around to gape at Myrtle. The cat bolted away as fast as she could go.

"Bad dogs!" snapped Myrtle sternly, brandishing her cane at them, towering over them with her full, nearly six-feet height.

The animals instantly put their tails between their legs and lowered their ears, whining at her as they slunk away.

Myrtle's police chief son lived directly across the street from her and his door flew open at all the commotion. "You okay, Mama?" he called.

"They weren't snapping at me—it was Pasha they were after. Now she's run off and I don't even know if she's hurt or not." Myrtle was exasperated at the note of panic in her voice. It was surprising how important that feral cat had become to her.

Red dodged back inside, finally hurrying out again with his shoes on. He strode purposefully across the street. "There *is* a leash law in this town. I sure wish folks would remember that." His once-red hair, now mostly gray, stuck straight up on one side of his head and his voice was rough and raspy as if he'd just awakened from a nap.

"You know how the old-timers are here in Bradley," said Myrtle. "They ignore whichever laws inconvenience them. These dogs don't have tags on them and I don't recognize them." She started calling for Pasha. "Kitty, kitty, kitty?" Her heart was still pounding and she breathed deeply to settle herself down.

"Pasha's too smart to come out before she thinks she's safe, Mama. Maybe after I've put these dogs in the police cruiser, she'll come." Red whistled to the dogs and then held out his hand and the animals obediently followed him as if he were the pied piper.

"Treats? For bad dogs?" Myrtle was outraged.

"They're just acting like dogs, Mama. Dogs chase cats. And I've got to get them into my car. I figured hot dogs would be certain to lure them in there."

Sure enough, the dogs were all over those bits of hot dogs. Once they were in the car, Red slammed the back doors and walked around to the driver's side.

"Well, I know you're not arresting them, so where are you taking them?" asked Myrtle.

"Just down to hang out at the station until someone claims them. That way I can also remind their owners about the leash law when they pick their dogs up," said Red.

Myrtle watched as he backed out of his driveway and then rolled down his window. "Mama, I'll help you look for the cat when I come back, okay?"

Myrtle raised her eyebrows in surprise. "I thought you weren't exactly Pasha's number-one fan."

"I'm not. Shoot, Mama, it's a feral cat. How am I supposed to feel about my octogenarian mother hanging out with a wild animal? But it's better for me to be stooping under bushes to look for her, instead of you. You're unsteady on your feet as it is."

Myrtle glared at him. He was interfering, as usual. "I'm just fine on my feet, Red. This cane just helps me move faster, that's all. It's really more of a fashion accessory than anything else. Go along to the station. I'll get Miles to help me."

He drove off and Myrtle reconsidered enlisting Miles's help. She decided to leave her friend alone for the time being. His guilty pleasure was watching her soap opera. She'd gotten him hooked on it, and it would just be wrapping up now. He'll actually know if Kayla escaped from the cult without consequence. Myrtle peered around her. "Kitty, kitty, kitty?" she called, bending down to look under bushes and neighbors' cars.

Which way had Pasha gone? Myrtle had to admit she wasn't sure, she'd just seen her run. Maybe she'd run far away, making sure she was well out of the way of those dogs. Myrtle walked back inside, opened a can of albacore tuna, and kept looking. After scanning her yard and her neighbors' yards, she moved down to the next block of houses, calling as she walked and hoping that the smell of the tuna might tempt the poor cat out of hiding.

The sun blazed down on her and the early-summer humidity felt oppressive. Myrtle thought she saw some movement in the bushes of a shady yard and walked right into the yard, calling and holding out the can. A squirrel scampered away and Myrtle gave a disappointed sigh.

She jumped a little as an authoritative voice barked, "Mrs. Clover. What are you doing?"

Myrtle looked up to see Rose Mayfield standing in her front door, hands on her hips, and an impatient look on her face. "I'm looking for my lost cat, that's all," said Myrtle. *Interfering biddy.*

"For heaven's sake. How will it help the cat if you have a heat stroke in my front yard?" Rose looked imperiously down her aristocratic nose at Myrtle. With her thin frame, brunette hair laced with gray, and angular features, middle-aged Rose had always reminded her of a particularly cranky Katharine Hepburn. "Come on inside," she said briskly, holding the door open. "Have some water, cool down, then you can find your pet."

"She's not a pet," said Myrtle as she walked in, sitting down on an antique sofa and carefully setting down her can of tuna. "She's a feral cat that I've befriended. Pasha's very sweet, despite being very wild."

"I'm sure she is," said Rose, cutting her off as she quickly walked into the kitchen, wet down a dishcloth with cool water, and handed it over to Myrtle. The look on her face indicated that *she* wouldn't allow *her* elderly mother to have a feral cat. "I'll get you some ice water."

Myrtle didn't like being lectured, but this time she bit her tongue and didn't argue with the authoritative Rose. That's because she discovered that she was actually, thirsty. She gulped down the water Rose brought her and then gave a begrudging apology for imposing, since Rose, arms crossed in front of her, looked so incredibly put out.

"Oh, it's fine," said Rose impatiently. "Your visit will distract me from the murder going on next door."

"Murder?" asked Myrtle with quickening interest.

As if on cue, a chorus of chainsaws roared to life.

Rose shuddered at the sound and her fingers tightened around her own glass of water. "That," she said loudly, over the racket. "That horticultural homicide. That woman next door is destroying all the trees and vegetation between our yards. Many decades of growth being felled and dragged away." Her face looked positively ill at the thought.

Myrtle paused as she tried to remember the neighbors on this street. "Let's see. Does Naomi Pelter live next door to you?"

Rose's mouth twisted with distaste. "That's the one."

"Why on earth would she want all the trees and shrubs taken away?" asked Myrtle, raising her voice over the buzzing chainsaws. The idea of losing the privacy that a densely-wooded lot provided was incomprehensible to Myrtle.

Rose shrugged. "Because she's insane?" she suggested in an acerbic voice. "When I asked her about it, Naomi had the silliest answer. Said that she hated raking and maintaining shrubs. Although I'm sure that *she* wouldn't be the one raking and trimming. Naomi always finds some man to do it for her, and it's usually a friend's husband—someone she's batted her eyelashes at. Wretched woman," she spat out. "I've considered lying down in front of the backhoe to stop the crew."

Myrtle took a thoughtful sip of her water. Before she could respond to this rather dire statement, however, Rose had changed course again. "Are you attending book club tomorrow?" she asked abruptly. "I'm hosting."

Myrtle set down her glass, sloshing water on her lap. She made a face and dabbed ineffectively at the spill with her napkin. She'd gotten to the point where she tried to miss as many book club meetings as humanly possible. The book picks were usually beach books with shallow plots and characters that all seemed very much alike. She silently fumed that Rose had put her on the spot. "I believe I need to work on my helpful hints column for the *Bradley Bugle* tomorrow, Rose."

Rose completely ignored this excuse as if Myrtle hadn't even made it. "You've got to come. Even if you haven't read the book, Miss Myrtle. I have a feeling that dreadful creature from next door is coming and I'll have to have someone else to talk to."

This statement shouldn't have enticed Myrtle to attend book club. But Naomi Pelter was becoming more intriguing. "She doesn't usually come to book club, does she? I've only remembered her there once or twice. What makes you think she'll make this one? Especially since you're clearly furious with her about cutting down all her trees."

"I think she'll be there because she needs to make up with everyone. She's on the outs with several members in our club. Maybe even with your Miles, Miss Myrtle." Rose gave her an amused look.

Myrtle laughed. "He's not *my* Miles. For heaven's sake. I must be fifteen years older than he is! Miles is a friend, that's all."

"Did you notice Naomi at the garden club luncheon yesterday?"

Myrtle's face flushed guiltily. She'd had an excellent excuse not to be at the luncheon but now couldn't remember her excuse for the life of her.

"Oh, missed that, too?" Rose arched her carefully plucked brows, giving Myrtle a reproachful look.

Myrtle thought she remembered that Rose was garden club president now. That would make sense, considering how upset she was about the trees and shrubs next door.

"We've had some wonderful speakers at garden club, you know. Truly wonderful. Last month, we had the guy from the county extension office to speak. He knew so much! He told us all about invasive plants, poisonous mushrooms, and garden pests." Rose clasped her hands together rapturously.

"The only garden pest I know of is Erma Sherman," said Myrtle grouchily. Her next-door neighbor was a member of garden club, but you couldn't tell it to look in her yard. It was all weeds: chickweed, honeysuckle, and crabgrass.

Rose ignored her interjection. "And yesterday, we had Timmie Watson tell us how she made a lovely flowerbed in a rocky, shady section of her yard. The annual luncheon was delicious, too, Miss Myrtle. And quite affordable."

The *affordable* part was delivered with a sidelong glance at Myrtle. It was irritating that the general public considered the elderly a mere step above abject poverty. A fixed income, even for a retired schoolteacher, wasn't exactly the end of the world...it simply provided Myrtle with a fairly strict budget.

Rose didn't appear to notice Myrtle's irritation. "Anyway, the only bad part of the luncheon yesterday was that Naomi chose to attend. In a large, floppy hat, nonetheless!" A flush crept up Rose's neck again. "The gall! Smiling and laughing as if she hadn't a care in the world. Yet she's eradicating all the trees and shrubs in her yard. Gardening, indeed!"

Rose currently seemed to be a one-topic hostess and, since Myrtle was tiring of the subject and eager to find Pasha, she pushed herself up out of her chair with her cane and said, "Most vexing, Rose, yes. Thanks for the water. I should keep searching for my cat now. Let me know if you see her, will you?" She reached over and picked up her can of tuna.

"Of course. You're coming to the book club meeting tomorrow, then?"

There was nothing more annoying than someone who was intent on an in-person RSVP. "I'll try," said Myrtle cautiously. The truth was that she'd lost all interest in book club as soon as they'd stopped trying to read actual literature. Right after the founding of the club, in fact.

Rose accompanied her to the front door. She made a face when she opened the door and hurriedly ducked behind it. "Naomi has come out to check on the work apparently, so I'll just let you navigate my front walk by yourself. You won't have any problems, will you?" She looked pointedly at Myrtle's cane.

"Not a bit," said Myrtle firmly as she walked away. Now she had a missing cat and a commitment to attend book club. It hadn't been the most productive of visits.

Naomi, wearing a sundress and a straw hat, was giving instructions to a very attentive crew. She spotted Myrtle and waved to her, walking away from the men. Naomi was in her early forties, but remarkably well preserved with a heart-shaped face and honey-colored hair. She took off a pair of very large round sunglasses to reveal sparkling green eyes. "Everything all right, Miss Myrtle?" She raised her eyebrows at the tuna can. "I saw you wandering through the yards a little while ago. Have you lost something?"

"My cat," said Myrtle. She thought she saw some movement in what remained of the natural area between Naomi and Rose's yards and bent to hold out the can. It was only a terrified bunny, though, trying to get away while the chain saws were quiet. Myrtle sighed.

"Sorry to hear that," said Naomi, although Myrtle got the feeling she hadn't really listened to what she'd said. Instead, she was staring at Myrtle's hair with an odd expression. Naomi abruptly reached out and smoothed down Myrtle's hair on both sides of her head. "I'm sorry," she said with a grin. "I couldn't resist. It was standing on end."

"Like Einstein's hair," said Myrtle. "It does that from time to time. Most annoying." She cleared her throat. "Are you going to book club tomorrow, by the way? Rose is having it, you know." Naomi looked blankly at her. Myrtle knit her brows. "Rose. You know—your neighbor?" Myrtle gestured to the brick house behind her.

Naomi made a face. "Oh, I don't think so, do you? What are we reading? Some sort of awful beach book, isn't it? Who wants to analyze *that*? How *do* you analyze that?"

Myrtle blinked at her. Sometimes she found kindred spirits in the most unexpected of places.

Naomi looked thoughtfully at Rose's house. "Maybe I should try to make it, after all. Mend some fences. I get the impression that Rose isn't pleased about the clearing I'm doing."

Apparently, Naomi wasn't particularly intuitive. Myrtle doubted Rose had been subtle.

Naomi nodded, "I'll plan on making it, then. Thanks for letting me know. And if I see your dog, I'll let you know."

Myrtle was opening her mouth to correct her when she realized Naomi was already gone.

Chapter Two

"Here kitty, kitty, kitty!" The shadows were getting longer now and Myrtle devoutly hoped that Pasha was simply hearing Myrtle's calls and not deigning to respond—that she was just being cat-like and not hurt...or worse.

She dropped the tuna can and made a face as it splattered all over Lula Franklin's driveway and Myrtle's sensible SAS shoes. "Shoot," muttered Myrtle. Then she called hopefully again, "Kitty, kitty?"

Unfortunately, the only response her call solicited was a gruff, "Hey, Mama."

She turned toward the street to see Red in his police cruiser. "No luck?" he asked, with a sigh.

Myrtle shook her head. She was furious at the tears pricking her eyes and gave a ferocious sniff.

"I was getting reports of a confused-looking elderly woman trespassing in yards and talking to herself. Figured I knew who it was," said Red.

Myrtle's tears instantly dried up. She glared at Red. "You made that up," she gritted out through her teeth. "Everyone in this town knows who I am...they would never have said *elderly woman.*"

Red put the car in park and walked around to hold open the passenger side door. "You're right. They said, 'Red, your mama has lost her mind and is trampling my marigolds.'"

"There are *no* marigolds in this driveway," protested Myrtle. Then she caught sight of a bed of rather flattened marigolds a couple of yards away and bit her lip. She walked to the car and carefully stooped to climb in and muttered, "Silly Lula. Those are zinnias, not marigolds."

Red got back behind the wheel. "I bet you don't have your cell phone with you, either."

She frowned at him and he continued, "I tried calling you earlier. You know, I'd feel a whole lot better about you off-roading through people's yards if I knew you had a phone to call for help if you fell."

Myrtle fumed. Mainly because she knew he was right and she despised his being right. It was very hard to get into the habit of carrying a cell phone around, though. "I left the house in a hurry, you know."

"Did you even lock your door?" asked Red with a sigh. "Never mind. I bet you didn't. Even if you did, did you call Dusty to ask him to help you replace that deadbolt on your back door? It's not sliding in right. Half the time I think you've got the door unlocked...even at night."

"He's put me on his schedule," said Myrtle. This, actually, was a bald-faced lie. She hadn't gotten around to calling Dusty yet, but she'd figured she'd just grab him when he came around to cut her grass. Trouble was, he hadn't mowed lately, either.

"All right," said Red dubiously. "If he doesn't fix it soon, let me know and I'll take care of it for you."

"I feel pretty safe anyway, Red. This *is* Bradley, North Carolina. Population fifteen-hundred. And you *are* the police chief."

"My job as chief fills me in on how *un*safe the town is. It's mostly piddly stuff, but a break-in is a break-in," said Red. He looked over moodily at her as they approached her driveway. "I feel as if I'm not doing right by you, Mama. You're going to end up with a serious injury and I'm going to feel guilty."

This conversation seemed to be moving in a direction that Myrtle didn't want to head in. She hurriedly said, "I'll start carrying the phone, Red. You're absolutely right."

Red blinked in surprise at the unexpected agreement from his mother. "I bet Pasha will come back tonight or tomorrow for sure. The dogs are out of her way now and she'll see that she doesn't have to hide. You'll see."

That night, Myrtle put a can of tuna outside. In the morning, it was gone.

Myrtle was bringing in the empty can when she saw a donkey-like face staring at her over the top of the fence and she nearly dropped the can. "Erma!" she snapped at her neighbor. "What are you doing up there? You scared me half to death." Erma always seemed to have some sort of excuse to be peering up over the fence. It was, in fact, a *privacy* fence. Unfortunately, it didn't seem to be affording her the privacy she most wanted.

"Oh, I had my stepladder out to clean some windows and thought I'd see what you were up to, Myrtle. You know how I

like to keep an eye out for you. I want to be a good neighbor."
Erma gave her a toothy grin.

"If you really want to be a good neighbor, you could do
something about that crabgrass," said Myrtle sternly.

Erma gave a braying laugh, revealing her large, protruding
teeth. "Myrtle, you crack me up. You really do. You're such a
character."

It was amazing that Erma was a devoted garden club member
and yet didn't give a fig about her yard.

Erma quickly changed tack. "Say. Are you going to the book
club meeting today? It's at Rose's house. We're discussing *The
November Choice.*"

Myrtle sighed. "I suppose so, yes." *The November Choice*
sounded like yet another book about a middle-aged woman trying
to jump-start her life after a divorce. She might have to bring
earplugs to use during the discussion.

"That's good. After you didn't make it to garden club, I was
getting worried about you. Maybe you had a cold, I thought.
That's why I'm checking on you now." Erma gestured down in
the direction of the stepladder. "My great aunt died from a cold,
did you know that? It went down into her chest and became
bronchitis and then pneumonia."

Erma had a great fondness for recounting medical detail and
had quite a memory for it. Myrtle tried to redirect her. Erma
was hugely annoying in almost every possible way—but she did
know a good deal of gossip.

"By the way, since we're talking about garden club and book
club," Myrtle hoped that she could redirect her in that direction,
anyway, "do you know much about Naomi Pelter? I ran into

her yesterday and realized I'd never really talked with her. What does she do?"

Erma grinned. "She bothers people. She flirts with women's husbands and asks them to do all kinds of favors for her—fix her stopped-up sink, clear out her gutters, mow her grass, do odd jobs around her house. And she seems kind of lazy. She doesn't have a job, even though she isn't married."

"How does she get any income, then?"

"Rumor has it that she has family money. They say that as long as she budgets sensibly, she should have enough cash for the long haul. Can you imagine?" said Erma wide-eyed.

Myrtle couldn't. She was too used to living on her social security and teacher's retirement.

"Do you remember when Naomi moved into town?" asked Myrtle, furrowing her brow.

"It was five or six years ago. Not long."

Myrtle nodded. "Interesting. All right, well, I've got to be going in now and have some breakfast. Pasha is missing, so if you see her around, could you let me know? Or maybe catch her and put her in your house and call me?"

Erma's face turned ashen. She was no fan of Pasha's—and vice versa. "Catch her? I'll probably just call you, Myrtle. Pasha and I don't ever get along. Besides, I'm allergic. I shouldn't have her in my house. That's why I have a goldfish for a pet. And Pasha probably wouldn't get along with my goldfish, either."

Myrtle nodded, waved, and started heading toward her door.

"See you at book club!" chirped Erma.

Myrtle's head started hurting.

That afternoon, Myrtle sat glumly in Rose Mayfield's carefully manicured backyard. She hadn't realized it was going to be an outdoor meeting when she'd worn her black slacks and long-sleeved yellow top. Now her color choice made her feel like another bumblebee in Rose's garden. She nodded to friend and neighbor, Miles, as he arrived clutching this month's selection. He appeared to take note of Myrtle's mood and avoided her by immediately going over to talk with an immaculately dressed Blanche Clark. Myrtle made careful note of where Erma Sherman was so that she could avoid her at all costs. She spotted her monopolizing a conversation with Georgia Simpson and quickly chose a chair far away from her.

The meeting was finally about to start after what seemed like an interminable period of socializing. "I don't see Naomi Pelter here," Myrtle said to Rose. This made Myrtle feel somewhat put out, since Rose had used Naomi as an excuse to get Myrtle to attend the meeting. And Naomi had told Myrtle that she was planning on coming to mend some fences with Rose over the landscaping kerfuffle.

Rose pursed her lips and said, "A huge relief, I must say. Naomi sent me an email from her phone yesterday evening saying she was very sick and couldn't come to book club. Naturally, if she's very sick, we don't *want* her at book club."

"That's the truth," said Myrtle. She was cursing the fact that she hadn't thought to use illness as an excuse, herself.

"I'm only hoping that there will be *no* chainsaw racket during our meeting. They seemed to be done with most of the cutting yesterday evening—I certainly hope that's the case." Rose's face grew mottled with emotion again. "It simply makes me sick to think about the poor trees and shrubs being annihilated over there. Perhaps, if it starts up again, I can get all of us to band together to protest. A protest would certainly be more effective with more people involved."

"Maybe she called off her landscapers, since she isn't feeling well," said Myrtle.

"Let's hope," said Rose fervently. She glanced at her watch and said, "I think it's time for us to start the meeting. I'm taking over as president for Tippy today, since I'm hostess and since she couldn't make it."

"Could I address the book club first?" asked Myrtle. "I wanted to make sure everyone knew about Pasha."

Rose looked at her blankly.

"My cat. You know," said Myrtle impatiently. For heaven's sake, that was the whole reason she'd been in Rose's yard yesterday. You'd think she'd remember.

"Oh. All right then," said Rose reluctantly. She gathered her skirts and sat on a metal folding chair.

Myrtle stood up and walked to the front of the assembled chairs. She cleared her throat and everyone gradually stopped their various conversations. "Before we get started," said Myrtle, "I wanted to make an announcement."

Everyone stared in surprise at her.

"It's my cat, Pasha," said Myrtle. "Well, she's not exactly *my* cat. She's really her own cat. She lets me feed her and pet her, you see." Everyone frowned in concentration as if trying very hard to understand. "Anyway, she's a black cat and she's missing. A gang of bad dogs chased her and I don't even know if she's hurt." She had to choke out the last few words and that made her furious. "Call me if you see her, please."

Now everyone was giving her sympathetic looks—even Miles, who Myrtle was sure had secretly despised Pasha since an unfortunate attack some time ago. She'd firmly believed Miles was in the wrong that time, though. Myrtle felt that prickling behind her eyes again and hurried toward Rose's back door for a tissue. Myrtle heard Rose saying behind her, "Well, I'm sure we'll all keep an eye out for the cat. Now let's move on to this month's meeting. There's other business to attend to before we discuss *The November Choice*."

Myrtle walked through Rose's porch to the back door and inside the house. The first thing she noticed was that Rose's front door was wide open. Myrtle frowned. There really were some squirrelly members in book club. You'd think someone would notice that they'd left a door wide open, though. No one had been raised in a barn that she was aware of.

She started toward the front door, and then froze at an acrid odor. Myrtle lowered her gaze...and spotted a very dead Naomi Pelter on Rose's hardwood floor.

Chapter Three

There was now no question that Naomi had been too ill to come to book club. The stench of a ghastly illness rose from her and her face in death still had found no peace. She wore a soiled tee shirt and cotton shorts and no shoes.

There sure hadn't been a dead body on Rose's living room floor thirty minutes ago when they were all greeted and told to assemble in Rose's backyard. Had Naomi felt desperately sick and come to book club for help?

Myrtle heard the back door open behind her as she stared at Naomi. Then she heard Miles's voice say, "Myrtle, are you okay? Rose sent me in to check on you. I have a clean tissue in my pocket ..." He stopped short.

Myrtle turned to look at him. Miles was staring in horror at Naomi, looking slightly sick himself. "What happened?" He pulled his gaze away and fastened it with relief on Myrtle.

"I guess she must have come in looking for help while we were outside," said Myrtle. "Rose said she'd emailed to say she was feeling sick and couldn't make book club."

"I'll say she was sick," said Miles, appearing a bit green. "I guess I should tell Rose and prevent anyone else from stumbling across this scene. Then we should call an ambulance or the funeral home or something." He quickly turned and walked toward the back door.

Myrtle stared thoughtfully at Naomi, remembering all the hard feelings against her. "You might want to call Red, actually."

"Red?" Miles turned around. "You're thinking this was foul play? Have you noticed how sick she looks, Myrtle? Maybe it's a natural death. She got terribly ill and then she died."

"Maybe. But that could be by design. Naomi had plenty of people who weren't very happy with her. Here comes one of them now," said Myrtle, nodding at the back door as Rose approached.

Miles groaned. "Rose isn't going to be happy about this. I'll call Red," he said, pulling out his cell phone.

Rose was unhappy indeed. Unlike Myrtle and Miles, she'd immediately spotted the body on her living room floor. Her eyes widened in surprise, and then displeasure quickly took over. She pressed her lips together tightly as she surveyed the scene, putting her hands on her thin hips. "Well, this is certainly inconvenient."

Myrtle could think of many other ways of describing it. "It's not as if she planned it, Rose. I think she must have walked next door for help, realizing how sick she was." Myrtle felt a pang of sympathy for the woman. She *had* been a proponent of Real Literature, after all. Perhaps the only one in the club who was, besides Myrtle and Miles. *The November Choice*, indeed!

Rose flapped her hand in the air impatiently. "Yes, I'm aware of that. But at this point, it's simply bad timing. I've got a backyard full of guests. Now I've got a dead body on the floor. Naomi had to crawl in like an animal to die? Typical thoughtlessness from that woman. Not only that, but my housekeeper, Sheila, has just recently quit and I haven't been able to find a new one. What am I going to do?"

Myrtle discovered that she didn't actually like Rose Mayfield very much. She said, "I heartily recommend my housekeeper. Her name is Puddin."

There was a strangled coughing sound behind her and they turned to see Miles there. Miles knew that Puddin was a hopelessly incompetent housekeeper in every way.

Rose frowned at Miles as if warning him that the coughing sound had better not indicate an illness...particularly considering the body on her living room floor. She then said to Myrtle, "Yes, if you don't mind, give me her number. Do you think she has any openings in her schedule?"

"Oh, I'm pretty sure she does," said Myrtle smoothly, as she reached in her pocketbook for a piece of paper and a pencil. "Miles, is Red coming?"

"He's on his way," said Miles.

"Red?" Rose's voice was cranky. "Why on earth is Red coming?"

"That's simply the usual procedure," said Myrtle. She'd made that up, but it *could* be the procedure. She jotted down Puddin's number and handed it to Rose. "Let's wait outside for Red," said Myrtle. "Besides, we need to tell everyone what's happened." She also wanted to watch everyone's faces when Rose told the book club the news.

Rose, Miles, and Myrtle rejoined the book club members, who had given up waiting and were instead, raucously visiting with each other and digging into the crustless party sandwiches and iced tea that Rose had provided. Rose cleared her throat and stood stiffly at the front of the group. No one even noticed. She cleared her throat again and still they loudly talked and laughed. Finally, she clapped her hands together and called out, "Everyone! Please!" and gradually the talking and laughter subsided. "If you could all take your seats again. There is something I need to tell you."

"There's been a–" Rose hunted for the right word. "Well, something has happened. Unfortunately, Naomi Pelter has expired on my living room floor." Her voice was somewhat exasperated. There was a gasp from the assembled group and Rose continued, "That's right. Naomi is inside now and I don't recommend that anyone go in there. Red is on his way over to assist us. She'd emailed me to say that she was ill and couldn't come to book club, and she was, indeed, ill."

Myrtle scanned the book club members' faces. Most looked shocked and concerned but there were a few interesting reactions, she thought. Rose, for one. She was more concerned about getting her house clean than about Naomi's death—but that was surely to be expected.

Myrtle also noticed that mousy Claudia Brown gasped and then looked terribly guilty. Myrtle remembered teaching Claudia many years ago. She'd thought her a fairly simple girl at the time and she didn't believe she'd acquired any higher thinking skills since then, either. Perhaps Claudia was only looking guilty because she didn't like Naomi and now has discovered that she's dead.

Lena Fowler, the Bradley vet, also had an interesting reaction. Myrtle watched as something of a satisfied smile crept across her face until she quickly removed it when she saw that Myrtle was studying her. Myrtle made a note that she'd have to find out more about Lena's thoughts on Naomi—and also get her to put a *missing cat* poster up in her office.

The last unusual reaction that Myrtle observed was Maxine Tristan's. She appeared positively delighted at the news of Naomi's demise. And when she heard that Red was coming over, she reapplied more blood-red lipstick and then powdered her nose.

To be fair, no one in the entire group seemed too broken-hearted at the news. Surprised, yes. But there were no tears shed over Naomi Pelter. This made Myrtle think that she hadn't been paying enough attention at past book club meetings. Was there all this anti-Naomi sentiment going on that she hadn't picked up on? Maybe she was losing her touch. Or maybe she should try to attend more book club and garden club meetings. Apparently, that's where all the action was.

Once Rose finished talking, the buzz of conversation picked up again, this time with an additional fervor. Myrtle decided she'd wait for Red on the porch. As soon as she'd opened the porch door, she saw Red entering through Rose's front door, so she walked into the house.

Red sighed when he saw Myrtle. "Mama, for once I'd like to have a body called into the station when you're not involved with it in some way." He turned his attention to Naomi Pelter. "Poor thing. She really was sick, wasn't she?" He knelt by the body and carefully studied her. "I wonder if she'd been sick for a while and maybe got dehydrated."

Myrtle said, "No, she wasn't ill at all until late yesterday."

Red glanced up at her. "You know that for a fact?"

"I do. I saw her yesterday afternoon when I was looking for Pasha. She talked to me for a few minutes and was even making plans for coming to book club. But at some point yesterday evening, she emailed Rose to tell her she'd become ill and couldn't make it."

Red said slowly, "So it came over her all at once?"

"Apparently so. Maybe it was food poisoning," said Myrtle. Then she paused. "Or maybe it was *real* poisoning."

"Why do you say that?" asked Red sharply.

"Because Naomi wasn't exactly winning any popularity contests in Bradley. I'm just saying that's a possibility. Are you planning on treating this as a natural death?"

Red shook his head and slowly stood up. "I'm planning on having the medical examiner make that call. She was pretty young to have died from a gastrointestinal bug, and in such a short amount of time. I've also got a call in to the state police. I think Detective Lieutenant Perkins is on his way now. If this needs to be treated as a homicide, we'll let them determine that." His eyes narrowed at her. "And this is all off-the-record. You're not planning on writing this up for the *Bradley Bugle*?"

Myrtle wrote a weekly helpful hints column for the newspaper, but sometimes wrote news stories for the *Bugle* when she had a chance and when her editor would let her. "That depends on whether this is real news or not. It might simply be a virulent virus or something." Actually, Myrtle was already planning on writing this story up, virus or no virus. Having something like this happen during a book club meeting was definitely newsworthy. Well, at least as far as Bradley's tiny newspaper was concerned.

"All right. And I'd like to keep it that way, Mama. If this ends up being a murder case...and I said *if*...then I want you to wash your hands of it." Red busily occupied himself with his notebook so he missed the look of irritation Myrtle shot him.

"Why ever not?" asked Myrtle. "What would be so special about *this* case?"

Red looked up from his notebook and directly into her eyes. "I *never* want you involved in a case. You know that. But this one would be different. The fact that it might involve folks in your book club, somehow. Friends of yours. It could get ugly and I don't want you involved in any ugliness. At your age, Mama, you should be thinking about relaxing—watching your soap opera, putting your feet up, and just resting."

Myrtle completely ignored this statement. This was Red's constant refrain. She'd gotten so that she really didn't even hear him when he said it. It sounded like *blah, blah, blah.*

"Now, if you could just step outside with everyone else, please. I've got to talk with Rose Mayfield for a few minutes before the medical examiner gets here." Red stood up from his crouching position with a wince. "Man, it's no fun getting old."

"I wouldn't know," said Myrtle airily as she walked out the back door.

The buzzing voices had quieted down to noisy whispers as Myrtle joined the rest of her book club. "Rose, I think Red wants to speak with you for a minute," she said.

Rose briskly walked to the house. Miles joined Myrtle. "Did Red give you an earful about discovering yet another body?"

Myrtle shrugged. "He mostly just wanted to warn me off of investigating."

"Doesn't he *always* warn you off of investigating?" Miles pushed his rimless eyeglasses up his nose.

"Red managed to find a slightly different excuse this time." Myrtle lowered her voice. "He said that this case might get messy, since the murderer would likely be a friend or a book club member."

Miles's eyes opened wide behind his glasses. "You mean, it *is* murder, then?"

"He won't know until after the autopsy I think. But I guess it could be, yes. The point is that he simply didn't want me poking my nose into the case and found a new excuse to latch onto."

Lena Fowler, the vet, joined them. She had the athletic build of a runner and cropped brown hair that suited her pixyish face. Lena also had a piercing, analytical gaze that always made Myrtle feel as if her slip were showing. "I was sorry to hear about Pasha, Myrtle. I remember when you brought her in to the clinic to get spayed and immunized."

Myrtle smiled at her. "I suppose you do, since Pasha wasn't in a very happy mood at the time."

Lena smiled back and Myrtle realized how infrequently a smile creased her serious face. "That was only to be expected. Feral cats would be even more worried about a cat carrier, car ride, and vet visit than housecats. She did a great job. I'll be sure to keep an eye out for her."

That uneasy feeling hit Myrtle again as she thought about Pasha. "Do you think she'll be all right? Do you think I'll get her back?"

Miles gave her that concerned look again.

"Was there a precipitating event that caused her to run off?" Lena's piercing gaze was back.

"There were dogs chasing her or snapping at her or something," said Myrtle with a sigh. "She looked terrified, but I couldn't tell if she was hurt."

"Sometimes cats will hide out for a while until the need for water drives them out. I wouldn't worry too much—she's probably fine." Lena's gaze flicked over from Myrtle to Rose's house. "Looks as if someone else has arrived."

"It might be the medical examiner," said Myrtle, also looking toward the house.

Lena frowned. "Does the medical examiner usually come for a natural death? Rose said that Naomi had emailed to say she was sick and couldn't make the meeting. Does Red think that this was foul play?"

Myrtle shrugged. "Who knows? Red never tells me anything."

Miles said thoughtfully, "I'd imagine that he has a responsibility to report a death like this." He pushed his glasses up his nose. "She was pretty young to have died so suddenly from a stomach bug."

Lena continued squinting at the house.

Myrtle said in what she hoped was a casual tone, "It's a pity, isn't it? I didn't really know Naomi as well as I should have, considering that she's a book club member."

"You weren't missing anything," said Lena coolly.

Miles and Myrtle shared a glance. "So you weren't close with Naomi?"

Lena snorted in response. "Hardly. But I'm not the only one who wasn't." She nodded her head to gesture around her. "Take a gander at Maxine Tristan. She looks positively jolly at this turn of events."

Myrtle remembered Maxine's grin at the news of Naomi's demise. Maxine was now engaged in conversation with another club member, but was grinning widely in response to everything said. She looked to be in a very happy mood.

"Am I missing something here?" asked Myrtle. "Is there a reason Maxine didn't like Naomi?"

"I'm not one to tell tales," said Lena briskly. "I only make observations." She raised her eyebrows as Red appeared at Rose's back door.

"He's going to want to speak to everyone," said Myrtle with a sigh. "And that always takes forever."

"I'm going to volunteer to talk with Red first because I really need to get back to the clinic. Hope Pasha shows up soon, Miss Myrtle." And she strode up to the house.

Chapter Four

The next morning, Myrtle ate her breakfast and then decided to walk over to the *Bradley Bugle* office. A blast of humid air hit her as soon as she opened the front door and she made a face—she'd hoped to avoid the heat by heading out so early.

Last night, she'd made a *Missing* poster with Pasha's picture on it and wanted to use the newspaper's copy machine to make a bunch of copies. Myrtle had realized at around midnight that she didn't have a really clear photo of Pasha on her computer and the pictures she *did* have were on her camera. She was going to have to get Red's or his wife Elaine's help getting the pictures off her camera, since she couldn't remember how she'd done it last time. Calling them at midnight, however, was not going to make them eager to help her. In the meantime, this poster would have to make do. She squinted at it. You could tell it was a black cat, she decided. Even though Pasha was running when Myrtle took the picture, turning her image into a bit of a black smudge.

Myrtle had put her cell phone number on the poster as the contact number and had even charged her cell phone last night.

It was now with her in the large pocketbook dangling from her arm. Red would be so proud.

Myrtle pushed open the old, wooden door to the newspaper and entered the cluttered newsroom. Once again, she smelled the musty-stale-paper-smell of the place. The room was filled with piles and piles of paper and photographs. Sloan Jones, the editor, claimed that he knew what every bit of paper in there was and could retrieve it whenever he needed. Myrtle had serious doubts about this.

Myrtle scanned the dimly lit room until one of the piles (or what she'd *thought* was one of the paper piles) moved on a wheeled chair to face her. It was Sloan, a hefty man with an ever-expanding forehead. He looked disappointed to see her. Their relationship was a little strained since Sloan was apparently rather terrified of Myrtle. He too-clearly remembered all the times she'd fussed at him in middle school for throwing spitballs and passing notes. You'd think that by the time he'd reached his forties, these memories would have faded. For Sloan, that didn't appear to be the case.

"Hi, Miss Myrtle." He gave her a grimacing smile. "Have you brought in your helpful hints column for me? That's awfully speedy of you. You must have read my mind. I know it's not due until later in the week, but if you've got it, I'll put it in tomorrow's edition. That's the most popular column we've got in the paper."

"No, I'm just here to borrow the copier. Pasha has disappeared and I need to put up some posters." She held up the mocked-up poster with the blurry picture of Pasha.

Sloan squinted at the picture. "Pasha?"

"You remember—the feral cat that took up with me?" Or was it that Myrtle had taken up with Pasha? "She's run off because of bad dogs and I need to make sure she's all right. As far as the helpful hints column—I might have to take a pass on it this week. There seems to be a bigger story looming on the horizon," said Myrtle.

Sloan began perspiring and pulled out a handkerchief from his pocket to blot his face. "Oh, is that the death of Naomi Pelter you're talking about? I don't think there's much story there, Miss Myrtle. Got sick, looked for help, died on the way to help. Sad, but no real story to report."

Myrtle studied him thoughtfully as he started nervously picking at the hem of his handkerchief. "Red's gotten to you, hasn't he?"

Sloan gave a rather high-pitched laugh. "I don't know what you mean, Miss Myrtle."

"Oh, I think you know exactly what I mean. Red came in or gave you a call and told you to warn me off this story. What I want to know is why," said Myrtle sternly.

Sloan quickly opened his mouth to argue the point, and then sighed, drooping a bit. "You nailed it. Red dropped by on his way to the station this morning and asked if I could divert you from following up on this story." He quickly raised his hands as if in self-defense as Myrtle started fussing. "But I don't know why, Miss Myrtle. I just assumed it was the same old reason—that he wants you to take it easy and stop chasing criminals around Bradley." He shrugged. "It's not a lot to ask, is it? You could take it easy, stay safe, and write your tips column for the paper."

Myrtle made a face.

"Folks love the tips column," Sloan said quickly. "You just wouldn't believe how often they tell me how much they *love* it. Boy, do they love to get those stains out of their clothes! Who has the money these days to throw out stained clothes? No sir, they want to get those stains out and re-use them. You're practically a hero, Miss Myrtle."

"Let me stop you right there," said Myrtle. "Enough of that nonsense. I've heard many more compliments on my in-depth articles on various murders in Bradley. We could train a chimpanzee to write those tips columns, but investigative journalism requires complex thought." She tapped a finger against her forehead.

Sloan's face fell. Myrtle headed to the copier and made twenty copies of her poster. She was sure that would give Sloan time to come up with some other fool's errand to try to send her on for the paper.

Sure enough, when Myrtle turned away from the copier, Sloan was holding a small box in his hands. "We got some promo freebies in the mail yesterday, Miss Myrtle. Want to do some write-ups for us? And you're welcome to take the stuff home, too. They might prove useful. Let's see. We've got a ..." he peered into the box and held up a thick-handled can opener meant to assist arthritis sufferers. "...helpful can opener that could be a lifesaver for our Bradley retirees."

Myrtle made a *pfft* sound. "I don't need one and don't want to write about it. I haven't a smidgeon of arthritis." She crossed her fingers at the fib. Her arthritis only acted up when it was rainy, so it was practically the truth.

Sloan sadly replaced the can opener in the box. "Will you at least have the tip column ready for me soon? I know it's due later in the week, but if you send it earlier, I can run it tomorrow even. It's pretty popular, as I mentioned."

It occurred to Myrtle that perhaps a small mention of her missing Pasha as a postscript to the column might be a good way to get the word out. After all, this was *The Bradley Bugle*, not the *New York Times*.

Sloan peered anxiously at her and then jumped as his office chair suddenly gave an ominous, squeaking groan beneath him. He stood up quickly, frowning at the chair suspiciously, as if it were the chair and not his weight that was at fault.

"Tell you what," said Myrtle. "I'll email the story to you later this afternoon." And she'd put a plea at the end of the story to watch out for Pasha. Maybe even include a photo.

Sloan blinked in surprise. "You will?" He looked concerned again. "We *are* talking about the helpful hints, right? Since you're not working on the Naomi Pelter story."

"Of course," said Myrtle smoothly.

"Where are you going now?" asked Sloan, apparently still not convinced that Myrtle meant to leave the story alone.

"Right now? I'm going to find my cat." She carefully slid her photocopies into the plastic grocery bag she'd brought with her and leaned heavily on her cane as she left. And if finding her cat meant running into a couple of suspects along the way, so be it.

Claudia Brown had certainly looked as if she had something to hide when she heard about Naomi Pelter's death. Myrtle hadn't imagined her guilty expression. Putting a missing poster near Claudia's house seemed in order.

Myrtle tacked up the poster on the stop sign at the corner where Claudia lived. Like most of the streets in Bradley, the stop sign was simply a suggestion to motorists. Most of the time, drivers only slowed down, hastily looked both ways, and kept right on driving. Hopefully, they'd also glance over Myrtle's poster with the blurry Pasha.

Unfortunately, Claudia didn't appear to be driven to do yard work today. Her blinds weren't even open on her house. Knowing Claudia and her usual bubbly personality, Myrtle found this a bit strange. Was she mourning Naomi? It seemed unlikely—no one was really mourning Naomi, at least as far as Myrtle could tell. Perhaps she should check in with Claudia and make sure she was all right. She could use Pasha as a cover. Besides, Claudia had seemed most concerned about Pasha when Myrtle had mentioned her disappearance at book club.

"Pasha?" Claudia squinted at Myrtle through her cat eye glasses moments later. "Who?"

Apparently, Claudia suffered from short-term memory loss. At least she showed the presence of mind to invite Myrtle inside. The day had really heated up and Myrtle was ready to enjoy a little air conditioning.

Except Claudia's house was fairly toasty. There was a small, oscillating fan in a far corner of the living room, lethargically swinging from left to right. "Air broken?" asked Myrtle.

"Oh no. I just get so chilly. You know."

Myrtle did *not* know. Especially in the summertime. But then, Myrtle had a very solid build. Claudia looked as though a small breeze might knock her off her feet. "Can I get you a cup of coffee?" she asked Myrtle.

Presumably to warm up. Assuming that no iced beverages were going to be offered, Myrtle said, "Thanks. With cream and sugar, please."

Claudia hurried to the kitchen, tightly-permed curls bouncing as she left. She was still talking in an aimless, filling-the-time kind of way, even though Myrtle couldn't make out the words over the listless whirring of the fan and the sound of a lawnmower from the house next door. There was lots of clutter on the sofa, chairs, and surrounding tables. Myrtle made a bit of room by stacking some of it and sat down on a weathered floral sofa to wait.

A few minutes later, Claudia returned with a cheery smile and two coffees, which she proceeded to slosh over the rim on her route to Myrtle. "There we are. Now, let's see. You came here to ask about someone named Pasha?"

"A cat. A black cat named Pasha. She's missing. I brought up the subject at book club," said Myrtle.

At the mention of book club, Claudia started anxiously pulling at her ear lobe. Myrtle longed to tell her to stop pulling at it, since her ears were certainly large enough without any stretching involved. She bit her tongue.

Claudia said slowly, "Oh. I've blocked out most of book club, I think. It was such a traumatic day, don't you think? So awful about poor Naomi."

"So you were a friend of Naomi's?" asked Myrtle. "You liked her? I'm only asking because she seems to have made some enemies along the way."

Claudia's face streaked with a red flush. "Naomi? She was...well, she was ..." She appeared deep in thought, trying to think of a kind word to use to describe the woman. Finally, she brightened after a silence, which was becoming painful for Myrtle. "She was talented! Yes, she was talented."

Then her face crumpled and she burst into tears.

Myrtle stared in horror at her, then quickly opened her gigantic pocketbook, fumbling around for the small packet of tissues that she could have sworn she'd put in there. She finally pulled out one that had a smudge of red on it.

"Sorry," she muttered. "It's clean, I promise. I only used it to blot my lipstick."

Claudia seemed to have no compunction about using the tissue, blowing her nose vigorously.

Finally, after what seemed like a lifetime to Myrtle, Claudia said, "I'm sorry. It's just hard for me."

Apparently, Claudia was a lot fonder of Naomi than Myrtle had thought. Maybe Myrtle had misread her expression when Naomi's death was revealed. Perhaps she'd been in shock or something.

But that explanation didn't *feel* right. It seemed to Myrtle that Claudia was not being completely forthright. And there were tears welling up again in Claudia's eyes again. Myrtle desperately jumped in.

"I suppose everyone felt the same?" asked Myrtle.

Claudia's eyes were confused behind the cat eye glasses.

"I mean about Naomi. Everyone joins you in feeling it's a great loss to the community?" asked Myrtle.

"Oh, no," said Claudia, shaking her head until the curls bobbed again. "I wouldn't say that *everyone* thought Naomi's death was a great loss to the community." She rubbed her cheeks, making them even blotchier. "Rose has said some dreadful things about Naomi. Really dreadful!" she reiterated, peeking out at Myrtle between her fingers as she rubbed her forehead.

"I suppose neighbors do tend to get upset with each other sometimes," said Myrtle, thinking of her own epic struggles with Erma Sherman. She was going to *have* to do something about that nasty crabgrass.

"I suppose so," said Claudia doubtfully. "It sure seemed like Rose was mad at Naomi, though."

"Anyone else? Someone besides Rose who might not have especially disliked Naomi?"

Claudia shifted in her seat uncomfortably. "Oh, I don't know. I sort of hate to say anything because I really don't know the whole situation."

"What whole situation?" asked Myrtle in as patient of a tone as she could muster. She plastered an expression of what she hoped looked like friendly interest on her face.

"Between Naomi and Lena." Claudia started picking at her fingernails. The woman was really a mess of nervous habits.

Lena Fowler had certainly looked rather relieved at the news of Naomi's demise, so maybe Claudia was on to something. The veterinarian had been on Myrtle's list of potential suspects to visit. "Lena didn't like Naomi?"

Claudia still focused on her nails. "I don't really know much about it, like I was saying. What I heard was that Naomi had asked Lena's husband to do a favor for her."

"What kind of a favor?" Myrtle leaned in a little. She was really expecting something salacious, so she was surprised at Claudia's answer.

"Naomi wanted Billy to climb up on her roof. I can't even remember what she wanted him to look at up there...maybe to see if the roof needed repairing, or to clean out her gutters. Or to adjust her satellite TV dish. It was some kind of chore she was asking him to do."

Myrtle said, "And Lena found out about it and drew her own conclusions?" She frowned. It didn't really seem to be in the vet's character to be unduly jealous over a favor.

"Oh, I don't know what Lena thought about it. She probably just thought that Naomi was such a flirt that she was able to convince Billy to get on her roof. But that's not the real problem, see. The problem is that Billy got up on the roof—and then fell off." Claudia stopped looking at her nails and finally met Myrtle's gaze.

Myrtle knit her brows, trying to remember. "You know, I think I do remember this. He wasn't merely injured, was he? He died."

Claudia nodded, permed curls bouncing vigorously. "That's right. And Lena blamed Naomi, since Billy would never have been up on a roof if Naomi hadn't asked him to."

Myrtle pursed her lips thoughtfully. Then she picked up her pocketbook and cane and carefully stood up. "Thanks for your help, Claudia. And thanks for looking out for Pasha, too. I appreciate it."

"Do you have a picture or anything? So that I'll know if I see her?" asked Claudia.

Myrtle handed her one of the flyers and Claudia solemnly studied it, and then put the flyer on her empty fridge door with a solo magnet.

"It's not the best picture," said Myrtle, "but hopefully it can at least help. I'm on my way to Elaine and Red's now to see if they can get better pictures off my camera. I've no idea how to do it. In the meantime, though, I thought I should put at least some type of notice up about Pasha."

"I'll keep an eye out for her," said Claudia. She gave Myrtle a clumsy hug. "I want to help."

Claudia was definitely one of those people who wanted to help...wanted to please. And softhearted too, if her reaction to Naomi's death was any indication. Although Myrtle, as she left, still had the feeling that Claudia was holding something back.

Chapter Five

"That's a picture of Pasha?" asked Red, peering at Myrtle's poster. "Can't say I'd have recognized her, Mama."

"That's exactly why I need you to help me pull some pictures off my camera," said Myrtle, reaching in her bag for her digital camera. "I swear, I don't know what good these things are if you can't figure out how to get the pictures off."

Red said, "It's just a matter of plugging it into the computer, opening the folder, and copying the pictures over to your computer. No big deal."

"Yes, well, I tried to do just that and I couldn't find the pictures. The camera seemed to have a bazillion folders on it." Myrtle tightly gripped the handle of her cane. She needed to be pleasant while asking a favor, but if Red were going to be condescending, it would be tough.

Red pulled the cable out of the zipper bag she'd put the camera and its assorted cords in. He started walking her through the process on his laptop. "First you plug this end into the camera and this end into the computer."

Myrtle gave him a forced smile when he glanced over at her.

"Then you wait for the computer to recognize the device." He paused. "Hmm. Maybe that port doesn't work for some reason." Red disconnected the cable from the laptop and plugged it back in at a different spot.

"Then, when the computer recognizes it, you click on the device on the laptop." He pointed to the icon, and then frowned. He leaned forward and studied the screen intently.

Myrtle felt smug. There were a dozen folders that popped up. How on earth would you know which one was the right one?

"Let's see," Red murmured. "It should be this one, I think."

It apparently wasn't.

Red said something rude to the laptop and the camera. "Maybe this is the right folder."

No, it wasn't.

Red's face was getting flushed now and he was randomly clicking on folders when his cell phone rang. With relief, he answered it. "This is Chief Clover. Excuse me?" he frowned, trying to listen harder. Then he rolled his eyes. "Yes. Thanks, Miss Brown. I'll let her know."

Myrtle sat up straight on the sofa. "Is it Pasha?"

"Sure seems to be. Claudia Brown is reporting a Pasha sighting." Red grabbed his keys and squinted at the poster. "You didn't put my number on the poster, did you? Hope I won't be getting a barrage of phone calls at the station about your lost cat."

"I can't help it if your citizens feel it's a police issue," said Myrtle. "Let's go!"

Elaine poked her head into the living room from the kitchen. "Was that call good news? Did you still need help with the camera?" she asked, looking down at the camera, laptop and cord.

"Maybe, just in case," said Myrtle. "But this sounds like a real lead."

It wasn't a real lead. "How on earth could Claudia think that cat looks anything like Pasha?" asked Myrtle impatiently. "It's just a common housecat. And it's fat as a butterball. Pasha is extraordinary."

Red gazed at the plump cat napping in a sunbeam across from Claudia's driveway. "Well, it is sort of hard to tell from your poster, Mama. Pasha looks more like a smudge."

"A blur," corrected Myrtle, coldly. "She was simply poetry in motion while I was trying to snap a picture." Myrtle sighed. "I guess Claudia was trying to help."

"I'll let her know that it was just a neighbor's cat and not Pasha. And Elaine will get a clearer photo off the camera. Since I'm busy with the case and everything," he added hurriedly, as if not wanting to admit that Elaine was better with computers than he was.

He and Myrtle climbed back into his police cruiser and Red started driving to Myrtle's house.

"About the case," said Myrtle. "So...it *is* a case. It's murder?"

Red looked irritated with himself for letting it out of the bag. "Yes, we're investigating it as murder."

"Naomi Pelter was poisoned then, I'm guessing?" asked Myrtle. "Considering how sick she was, I mean."

Red sighed. "Yes."

"What type of poison was it? Nightshade? Foxglove?" Myrtle tried to sound brisk and efficient—one crime-fighting colleague having a conversation with another.

Red said, "In what capacity are you asking these questions? As Myrtle Clover, concerned book club member? Myrtle Clover, ace reporter? Or Myrtle Clover, amateur detective? I really don't want you getting involved in this, Mama. I think we might be dealing with someone fairly dangerous."

"Isn't that to be expected, considering that we're talking about murder? And, to answer your question, I'm a concerned book club member, of course. Nothing more."

Red paused. "All right. Since I'm sure this information is about to be released to the public, I'll fill you in. She ate poisoned mushrooms."

Myrtle grimaced. "Not a very nice way to go, is it? Was it a particular type of mushroom?"

"It's called Destroying Angel, apparently. It's supposed to look very much like an ordinary button mushroom."

"Wouldn't it taste awful?" asked Myrtle, wrinkling her nose at the thought.

"Apparently not. The experts were saying it's very bland. So, there's nothing that would stop the victim from eating them," said Red.

"Does the poison start working right away?"

"No, they said that you'd be fine at first. Then later, you'd start having what seemed like a really bad stomach virus. If you don't get help, though, it acts pretty quickly. The victim ends up delirious," said Red, looking grim.

Myrtle mulled this over for a moment. "So Naomi probably thought at first that this was something that she could simply self-treat. A bad tummy bug. By the time she needed help, she probably wasn't even making sense anymore."

"That's what I understand," said Red. He pulled the cruiser into Myrtle's driveway.

Myrtle had heard something about mushrooms recently, she was sure of it. If she could only remember when. She heard so much pointless blather that didn't seem significant at all—until suddenly, it was.

It was right after *Tomorrow's Promise* ended that Myrtle decided to check her emails. As usual, she had about fifteen spammy emails promising her riches if she'd only share her bank account number with a stranger in Nigeria. She snorted. Were there people who actually believed that stuff? And the emails always started out "Greetings dear one" in all caps. Awfully chummy, to be coming from a complete stranger.

Then she blinked. Right in the middle of the spam was an email from Elaine...with what appeared to be an attachment of a photo. Myrtle quickly clicked on it and brought up a very handsome photo of Pasha, who gazed imperiously at the camera. It was perfect. Myrtle carefully clicked on the picture, made it larger, and printed it.

After a return visit to the *Bradley Bugle* office, where Sloan made sure he was very busy on a phone call during her entire time there, Myrtle revisited the spots where she'd put up the old posters and covered them with the new one.

Myrtle was breathless afterward. Clearly, the heat was the culprit, not the mile or so she'd walked. She glanced around for a good spot to rest, but was surrounded by residences. Fortunately, there was a pickup truck parked on the street. It had a bumper generous enough to prop herself up on for a short spell. She leaned on her cane and gingerly perched on the truck's bumper.

The sun beamed brightly into her face and she closed her eyes. A few moments later, she heard a car drive close...and then stop in front of her on the road. She opened her eyes, shielding her face with her hand and saw Miles looking curiously at her from the window of his Volvo.

He lowered the passenger side window. "Everything all right, Myrtle?" He pushed his glasses a bit higher on his nose and peered at her with concern. "Too much sun?"

"Too much heat, I think," said Myrtle, trying to sound careless. "It's *always* affected me like this." *Being an octogenarian had nothing to do with it.*

"Are you done handing out the posters? Or would you like a ride to put more out?" asked Miles. "I guess there's no sign of Pasha so far."

Miles sounded a bit reluctant to help with the great Pasha search.

"Don't trouble yourself," said Myrtle coldly. "I'll simply rest a moment and then walk to my next destination. It should only take me twenty minutes to get there."

Miles gave her a stern look. "Absolutely not. Don't be silly, Myrtle. Hop on into the car. I've got air conditioning."

"Is that akin to puppies and candy? I was told not to get into a car with anyone promising treats." Myrtle was feeling remarkably contrary.

Miles set his jaw and reached all the way across the sedan to push open the door for Myrtle. She finally climbed in, clutching her posters carefully.

Miles appeared to take a couple of deep, calming breaths as they set off. "Where to? Are we just going to random lampposts and putting up posters?"

"If we see a good spot. But I think I've covered most of the best places already. I was thinking that I should head out to Lena Fowler's clinic. They always say it's a good idea to put flyers up at a vet's office," said Myrtle.

Miles thought about this. "Do you and Lena Fowler know each other well?"

Myrtle looked over at him with a frown and Miles continued, "She seems like she's difficult to get to know. I've tried to strike up a conversation with her at book club a few times, but my attempts always seem to peter out."

"No, I wouldn't say that I've had much small talk with Lena," said Myrtle. "But I do have a cat. You don't have a pet at all. Lena would have something to talk with you about if you had a dog or a cat or even a bird or turtle or something. She's the type who gets along better with animals than she does with people."

"She's somewhat intimidating," murmured Miles. "Sometimes I see her out running."

"Jogging, you mean?"

"No, I mean running. She's so intense. There's no *jogging* about it. The woman looks as if she's fleeing from a bank robbery or something. It's startling," said Miles.

"Maybe she *is* running away from something—metaphorically speaking," mused Myrtle. "She was supposed to be very upset about her husband's death. Maybe she's trying to put some emotional distance between herself and her feelings for her husband."

"Or maybe she's just one of those exercise nuts," said Miles dryly.

Myrtle ignored this and continued verbally working it all out. "As a matter of fact, I did want to talk to Lena about Naomi's death. Lena had a very satisfied look on her face when we announced what had happened at the book club meeting. I'm sure there's a story there. And I believe it has to do with her husband's accident."

Miles stared at her, and then snapped his head back to look at the road again. "It sounds like you're trying to investigate Naomi's death. But Red didn't say it was murder, did he?"

"Miles, I'll have to fill you in later," said Myrtle as Miles pulled the Volvo in front of the vet's office. "But yes, it was murder."

Myrtle and Miles walked into the small waiting room. It was empty in there, which Myrtle knew from experience was unusual. The receptionist looked up from the muffin she was eating and quickly wiped her mouth with a napkin. "Can I help you?"

"I just wanted to put up a poster for my missing cat on your bulletin board and talk with Dr. Fowler for a minute. Is she in?" asked Myrtle.

"She is. We just had a couple of hours of quiet, although it looks like our afternoon is booked solid. There are some extra pushpins on the board if you want to go ahead and put the poster up. I'll ring Dr. Fowler in the back." The receptionist picked up the phone.

A few minutes later, Lena Fowler ushered them back into the clinic. She was lean and a good deal shorter than Myrtle. She was built like a runner and Myrtle's cane thumped regularly on the floor as she hurried to keep up with her brisk pace toward the back. There was no one in the clinic, so why was Lena so impatient?

"I know you'd recognize Pasha, Dr. Fowler," said Myrtle rather breathlessly as they reached her small office, "so I wanted to remind you to be on the lookout for her. I mentioned it at the book club meeting, but thought you should know that I haven't found her yet."

Lena's intelligent brown eyes softened a bit at the mention of Pasha. "I'm so sorry to hear that, Mrs. Clover. Of course, I'll keep looking for her. But I wouldn't worry too much about Pasha, although I know it's tough not to. She's a survivor."

Something in Lena's expression made Myrtle say, "You are too, aren't you? I know you've had a rough time yourself lately."

Lena stiffened. "I wouldn't say *lately*, Mrs. Clover. Things are going well at the office. And I do have friends. But yes, it was very hard when I lost Billy a couple of years ago. You're a widow yourself, so I'm sure you understand."

Myrtle nodded sagely, although she'd been widowed about thirty years ago and the memories had faded quite a bit. "Miles is, too." Miles blinked at her and she corrected, "Rather, Miles is a widow*er*."

Miles gave an uncomfortable smile and cleared his throat. "It doesn't really get any easier, does it?"

It was the kind of thing you say when you're not really sure what to say and you simply want to fill an awkward pause. But it clearly created a reaction from Lena.

Lena blinked hard and turned away slightly to quickly swipe at her eyes. She said gruffly, "That's the truth. Especially when it's such a pointless death. There was no reason for Billy to have died that day."

Myrtle said slowly, "Lena, remind me again? I'm so sorry—my memory isn't what it should be these days—but was it something to do with his doing a favor for a friend?"

"Some friend!" Lena said with a snort. "Naomi Pelter, you mean? If she'd been a true friend, she'd never have asked Billy to get up on her roof. She was supposed to have some money of her own...she should have paid someone to clean her gutters, like everyone else does. But the silly fool was taken in by her batting eyelashes and next thing you know, he was a goner. He never did have a great sense of balance," she ended with a laugh that sounded closer to a sob.

Miles gave Myrtle a desperate glance. He was never fond of emotional scenes. When Myrtle had gotten him hooked on her soap opera (something he had made her promise never to mention to others), she'd noticed that he peeked out between his fingers whenever there were tear-jerking scenes.

Lena, though, seemed much too strong to fully break down, especially in front of visitors to her office. She quickly regained control. "As you mentioned, it takes a while to recover from the death of a spouse."

Myrtle worried they were about to be dismissed and hurried on, "So true. And a sudden death only makes it worse, don't you think? Like Naomi's death at book club. Shocking!"

Lena frowned at Myrtle. "Well, clearly, I'm not too broken up at Naomi's sudden death, Mrs. Clover. I didn't wish her harm, per se, but I'm not going to fake grief either. It did appear to be an unpleasant death. I'm assuming she became dehydrated and that that was a major contributing factor to her demise."

"Actually, Red just told me that it wasn't a mere stomach bug that she had," said Myrtle, carefully studying Lena. "It was murder."

Lena's expression was guarded again. "He's sure about that? Well," she looked away from them. "I didn't like the woman, but as I mentioned, I didn't wish her any harm."

Miles said, "I'm sure you weren't the only one in town who didn't care for Naomi."

Myrtle added, "There were quite a few, I think. At least that was the impression I got at book club."

Lena nodded, absently smoothing down a stray lock of hair. "There were. Our book club hostess, for one. She was blasting Naomi every chance she got. Rose was furious at Naomi for cutting down all those trees and bushes."

Myrtle murmured, "And someone was telling me something about Maxine Tristan, I think. Although I don't exactly know what she was alluding to."

Lena rolled her eyes. "Well, I think it has to do with the fact that Maxine saw Naomi as competition. But I wouldn't want to gossip." She looked down pointedly at her watch, although there wasn't anyone waiting.

Myrtle ignored the fact that Lena was trying to get rid of her. Sometimes people thought older folks were clueless about social cues. She'd just allow Lena to believe that for a moment. "Red is trying to track down who might have been around Naomi in the days prior to her death," she said. Well, she was sure he *was*, even if he hadn't shared that tidbit with her. "Did you see Naomi recently?"

"If I had, I'd have glanced away and kept walking," said Lena dryly. "Besides, I was out of town at the other times I'd have normally seen Naomi. I'd missed the garden club meeting last month, and, although I made the annual luncheon, I was seated far away from Naomi."

"I see," said Myrtle. She paused for effect, but the only effect appeared to be the fact that Lena looked impatient. "Do the words *Destroying Angel* mean anything to you?"

Lena frowned. "That's a poisonous plant of some kind, isn't it?"

"That's right—a mushroom," said Myrtle.

Lena nodded. "I have heard about it. Destroying Angel has been known to kill dogs before, as I recall...that's why I know about it. The mushrooms can grow on tree roots and dogs eat them and the ingestion is always fatal. I do know a bit about poisonous plants because pets sometimes eat things that they shouldn't." She narrowed her eyes. "Are you saying that's what killed Naomi? A mushroom?"

"I believe that her cause of death is likely still under investigation," said Myrtle a bit cagily. Miles gave her a worried look. All they needed was for word to get back to Red that Myrtle was questioning suspects about mushrooms. This time, Myrtle was the one who was impatient to leave.

Chapter Six

That night, Myrtle set out more canned cat food in the backyard. She was sleepy enough to fall asleep straight away, but by two o'clock, she was staring at the ceiling, completely awake. What was there that was so familiar about mushrooms? Why the odd sense of déjà vu?

Her eyes opened wide. She knew exactly where she'd heard it before. She shoved herself out of the bed, stuck her feet into a pair of tennis shoes, and threw on her robe. Surely Miles was awake tonight. After such a stimulating day, who could sleep?

She was right. Miles's lights were on. She hurried up his walkway and rapped on his door. Miles, dressed in plaid pajamas under a navy bathrobe, opened the door right away as if he'd been expecting her. "Hi, Myrtle," he said calmly.

"Hi, Miles."

Miles led the way to his kitchen where he already had two cups and saucers out and a coffeepot carafe sitting on a trivet on the kitchen table. He was already pouring exactly the right amount of half-and-half in her cup and putting in a loaded teaspoon of sugar before pouring coffee on top, stirring, and passing it wordlessly her way.

Myrtle took a couple of sips and nodded in approval, waiting as Miles fixed his own cup. "Got any cookies?" she asked, glancing around his kitchen.

He reached for a plate that was hiding behind the coffeepot. Myrtle took a chocolate chip cookie. She raised her eyebrows. "Homemade?"

Miles shook his head. "Just like homemade according to the package. Homemade by somebody, I guess."

Myrtle nodded. She said, "Miles, I made a discovery."

"I rather thought you might. You seemed deep in thought on the way back from the vet."

"I'd heard from Rose that the latest garden club meeting featured a speaker from the county extension office who talked, among other things, about poisonous mushrooms!" Myrtle sat back in the chair and beamed at Miles.

Miles seemed slow to take this news in. "So, do you think that Rose is responsible...?"

"No, no. At least—well, she might be. She was at the garden club meeting, after all. But so were other suspects in this case. Claudia is a garden club member; Maxine goes to garden club ..."

"Aren't you a garden club member?" asked Miles, wrinkling his forehead.

"Officially, I'm on the roster," said Myrtle with a shrug. "I'll go if there's nothing else to do. Although I've gotten rather discouraged with my situation and haven't felt like hearing all the wonderful things I could do with my yard."

"What's your situation?"

"Erma Sherman and her crabgrass. I'm in the trenches, fighting a war with crabgrass, and can't devote any of my time to frippery like impatiens or gardenias," said Myrtle.

"But you weren't at *that* meeting," said Miles. "So you don't know exactly what took place."

"No, I'll have to ask people about it. You see, there were a couple of meetings that I missed. One was the regular meeting with the speaker from the extension office. The other was the annual luncheon. So the murderer could have found out about Destroying Angel mushrooms at the meeting and then had the opportunity to poison Naomi with them at the luncheon. And it makes me very irritated that I didn't make it to either one," said Myrtle, now feeling grouchy.

Miles took a sip of his coffee. "Lena Fowler wouldn't have been at that garden club meeting though, right? She'd mentioned being out of town."

"She did," said Myrtle. "But she also told us that she was familiar with Destroying Angel mushrooms because of her research into poisons that affect family pets. Remember? So this is something she could have come up with on her own without having attended garden club."

"Doesn't that seem like a coincidence though?" asked Miles. "That she would happen on that very method of poisoning Naomi, right after the garden club meeting that mentioned it?"

"That's what makes it the perfect poison, though. By using Destroying Angel mushrooms, Lena could make it appear as though the garden club members might be responsible...and, conveniently, she was out of town for that meeting," said Myrtle. "Maybe she even heard a garden club member chatting about the meeting at her clinic and realized that would be the best way to finally get rid of Naomi. Or maybe she read the minutes from the last meeting—they're always listed online."

"She certainly still seemed to carry a grudge," said Miles thoughtfully. "It's something to consider, for sure. Do you think Red has already heard that that was a topic at the meeting?"

"I hope not. That gives me some time to question some of those women before he catches on. As far as he knows, I'm just trying to interact with them because of garden club business." She finished her coffee and pushed it away so that she could lean her elbows on the table. "Could you drive me somewhere to-morrow?"

Miles was cautious. "Where?"

"Just somewhere too far for me to drive. I have an errand," said Myrtle carelessly. Miles wouldn't want to drive her if he knew where she was going.

"You're not going to that psychic's house, are you?" he asked suspiciously.

Myrtle blinked at him. "Are you psychic yourself? Maybe it runs in the family." She hid a smile. Miles had been shocked to discover that the local psychic Wanda and her brother Crazy Dan were cousins of his. Shocked and discouraged.

"Why do you want to go see that old charlatan?" asked Miles with a groan. "She spends her days cheating the gullible out of their hard-earned cash."

"You're simply still reeling from the fact that you're cousins," said Myrtle with a sniff. "If you don't want to go over there, just let me borrow the car. Wanda may be rough around the edges, but she has great insight and intuition." She gave a little shiver. Sometimes Wanda was spookily on target.

"Rough around the edges? Wanda is rough all over. I think you're fascinated with her because she keeps giving you these dire prophesies. You're like a deer in the headlights," said Miles.

"Like I said, if you don't want to go, just let me borrow your Volvo. Come on, Miles—what are friends for?" She gave him a pleading look.

"All right," said Miles in a grouchy tone. "I suppose we can go tomorrow afternoon. I'm going to bring my hand sanitizer, though. Crazy Dan and Wanda's home could use some spring-cleaning. Summer, fall, and winter-cleaning, too."

Myrtle was already on another topic. "Could you look up Destroying Angel on your computer? I still don't have a great grasp on how that stuff works."

Miles pushed his chair back and went off to get his laptop. He signed in, pulled up a search engine, and typed in the name of the mushroom. He squinted at the screen. "No information."

"That doesn't sound right." Myrtle got up and walked over to look over Miles's shoulder. "It's apparently a serious poison. There should be tons of information on it." She leaned over far enough so that she nearly lost her balance and toppled over on him. Miles helped her regain her balance and she leaned back on her cane for support. "Oh, for heaven's sake. Miles, you put in Destroying *Angle*, not Angel."

"No wonder," muttered Miles.

"Destroying Angle—the scourge of Geometry!" Myrtle grinned.

"All right, all right," said Miles, even more grouchy. He quickly corrected the search term and the screen pulled up white, leggy mushrooms in what was apparently a variety of different maturity levels for the fungus. "It's actually a fairly attractive thing, isn't it?"

"Especially considering how deadly it is," said Myrtle. She skimmed the page. "It looks like a victim doesn't immediately get sick. It might be five or even twelve hours after ingestion."

"Ugh," said Miles. "And after a while, the symptoms stop for a while and the victim might think he's getting better and skip seeking help."

"Which is a mistake," said Myrtle. She gave a low whistle. "The symptoms start getting worse again and at that point it's too late."

Miles ran his finger along the text. "Kidney failure. Liver failure. Awful."

They stared silently at the screen. "Not a nice way to go," said Myrtle quietly.

"I wonder if the person from the extension service explained how the poison worked," said Miles. "Somebody must have been really upset with Naomi to have done this."

When Myrtle finally headed back home, she was ecstatic to discover that the food she'd set out for Pasha was gone. She stooped down, looking under bushes in her dark yard and calling out softly to the cat. She didn't see Pasha, but she saw that crabgrass was creeping over into her yard inch-by-inch.

Like an avenging angel, Myrtle stormed into her house, reached under her kitchen sink, and pulled out a large container of homemade weed killer. Since she lived on the lake, she was always mindful of runoff of the poisons into the water and had determined to use safe, organic products. Not only that...well, it was a lot cheaper than buying the commercial weed-killers. This one worked like a charm and was composed of a gallon of apple cider vinegar, a half-cup of table salt, and a teaspoon of dishwashing detergent. The only problem was lugging the thing around, so she'd distributed it into smaller spray bottles after mixing the stuff up.

Myrtle hurried back outside with the spray bottle and set it down beside the fence. She was glad to be six feet tall sometimes, although it had felt like a curse when she'd been young. She couldn't really *see* what she was spraying, but it didn't matter since Erma's yard was consumed by crabgrass. She pumped the spray bottle and covered as much area as she could reach from her position. That was as good as she could do, considering it was the middle of the night. Then she put out some more food for Pasha and finally turned into bed.

The next morning, as Myrtle walked out to get her newspaper, she noticed that Erma's yard smelled like a salad. She smiled to herself. Perhaps, if Erma left the house later, she might find the opportunity to destroy the rest of the weeds in her yard. Erma was such a poor garden club member that she might accept that it was some sort of odd blight.

After eating a grapefruit and some toasted oat cereal, Myrtle planned out her day. She had the trip to see Wanda this afternoon with Miles. But what should she do this morning? She thought about it. It seemed to her that all roads appeared to lead to Rose. Rose was the one with the grudge against Naomi. Naomi's body was discovered at Rose's house. Rose was at the garden club meeting that mentioned Destroying Angle...and at the luncheon where she could have given it to Naomi. Red's warning voice popped into her brain, unbidden. Myrtle grabbed a Pasha flyer and her cane and pushed open her front door—right into Miles.

"Sorry," said Myrtle. She frowned at Miles. "We weren't going to see Wanda this morning were we? I thought we'd arranged it for the afternoon."

"You're right," said Miles quickly. "I just thought I'd accompany you to your next suspect interview. For...support."

Myrtle gave him a suspicious look. "Support." She glanced across the street and caught sight of Red giving Miles a rather jaunty wave. Why did she have the feeling that Red had called Miles and asked him to provide *literal* support for Myrtle? Irritating. Especially today when she was *particularly* steady. She had half a mind to fuss at Miles about it—except she didn't have any proof. Besides, she did want her sidekick to come along with her. Sometimes he caught things that escaped Myrtle's attention. "All right," she said a bit ungraciously. "Here, you can hold the flyer. That will be our excuse for going there."

"To Rose's house?" asked Miles. "She's your prime suspect right now, right?"

"Currently," said Myrtle. "Although that's always subject to change."

Rose was, as expected, not particularly pleased to see them. "Oh, hello," she said. She homed in immediately on the flyer. "Is this for me?" she asked. She took the flyer out of Miles's hand without being offered it. Her hooded eyes glanced over the flyer. "Missing cat. Oh. That's the animal you were talking about earlier, isn't it?" she asked Myrtle, her willowy frame standing ramrod straight.

Myrtle, despite leaning over on her cane still held a height advantage. "Pasha. The cat's name is Pasha. I wanted to bring you a flyer to help you look out for her. I figured, since you were such a nature and animal lover, that you would be a good candidate to help find her."

Rose gave her a stern look. "Animal lover? How do you figure that?"

Myrtle tried to hold her irritation in check. She bared her teeth in a smile. "All your talk of nature and loving your trees and shrubs, of course."

"You made the leap that I was an animal lover simply because I like trees?" Rose pressed her lips together.

At this point, Myrtle despaired that the gatekeeper would allow them entry into her home, but Miles cleared his throat and said, "Rose, if you don't mind, could we come in for a moment and sit down? Myrtle's balance, you know." He looked suggestively at Myrtle and Myrtle was appalled to feel herself take a small step backward to keep upright. The power of suggestion was a terrible thing.

Rose sighed and opened the door wide. Myrtle walked through her entrance hall and along the hardwood floors to Rose's living room, waving Miles's hand away as he reached out to her for support when she stepped onto the various scatter rugs over the wooden floors. She dropped down onto a sofa that looked a great deal more supporting than it actually was. It dissolved into a downy *poof* and she sank deep into the bowels of the sofa. She gripped her cane tightly. She'd be hanged if she'd ask for help from Miles or Rose to escape Rose's furniture.

Myrtle decided that it was time to take control of this conversation. "So you were saying that you weren't technically an animal-lover, Rose. But you were very upset about Naomi cutting down the trees between your yards."

"Naturally I was. Naturally. And I don't mean I won't look out for your cat. Of course I will. But my concern has always been primarily with protection and preservation of natural areas," Rose plucked in an agitated way at the cuff of her stiffly starched white blouse. Myrtle noticed that when Rose was stressed that her dimples flashed. It was most distracting.

"Something that Naomi Pelter didn't understand," prompted Myrtle.

"Exactly," said Rose sharply.

"In fact," said Myrtle softly, "Naomi got what she deserved."

Rose opened her thin mouth quickly to agree, and then hesitated. "Perhaps. I am a believer, Miss Myrtle, of karma. What goes around comes around."

Myrtle narrowed her eyes. She didn't need karma defined for her. It was annoying when people thought she was simple-minded. Miles appeared to be giving her a steadying look.

"Naomi didn't consider others. And now, she's gone." Rose shrugged a thin shoulder. "I believe people who put bad things into the world take bad things out of it."

Mumbo-jumbo.

Myrtle was staring out across the room, trying to tame her tongue when she caught sight of something black looking in at her through Rose's French doors that lead out into her backyard. Pasha!

Myrtle thumped frantically across Rose's floor to the French doors, flinging them open with abandon and hurrying out into Rose's backyard, calling for the cat, which had suddenly evaporated into thin air.

She could hear Rose fussing about her behind her. "What on earth possessed her? My doors could have splintered into a million pieces the way she threw them open like that. And she didn't even shut them behind her. Was she raised in a barn? Besides, I thought you said that Miss Myrtle was unsteady. And she just sprinted off like that!"

Miles gave Myrtle a sympathetic look as she turned and walked toward them. "No luck?" he asked.

"Must have been a shadow. A trick of my eyes or something," muttered Myrtle.

"I'll have to check my doors for damage," said Rose in a shrill voice.

Myrtle leveled a look at her that should have been able to curdle cream. "By the way," she said pointedly, "Naomi's death was murder. And you don't seem to have been Naomi's greatest friend. In fact, you could easily be considered her greatest enemy."

Rose rubbed her bony temple as if it were starting to pound. "I had nothing to do with Naomi's death."

"It seems as though you had plenty to do with it. For one, you *hosted* her death. She chose to crawl in your house to die." Myrtle continued staring grimly at Rose.

Rose looked away first. "That's a very strange way of putting it, Miss Myrtle. I certainly didn't invite Naomi Pelter over here to pass away. I've no idea why she would have possibly chosen to spend her last remaining moments on the floor of my living room."

No, Myrtle could see that was the case. Rose Mayfield didn't possess the imagination to envision why Naomi would have ended up here.

Miles said mildly, "Don't you think that she probably realized you still had guests here, had an unlocked door, and would be available to help her?"

Rose just stared blankly at him. "All I know is that I had nothing to do with Naomi's death. I guess everyone thinks I did it," she said stiffly. "Or at least *some* people think I did it." Here, she gave Myrtle a cold glare. "But I didn't."

"Do you have any idea who might have wanted Naomi dead?" Myrtle asked.

"If you can't say something nice, don't say anything at all," said Rose, sticking her thin chin into the air. "That's what my mother taught me."

Rose rather inconsistently observed this rule, considering that she was bad-mouthing Naomi over the deforestation only days earlier, Myrtle thought.

When Rose's cold glare grew another thirty degrees frostier, Myrtle realized she'd said those words out loud.

Chapter Seven

The rather uncomfortable interview with Rose had made Myrtle oddly hungry. She persuaded Miles to go to Bo's Diner with her before they headed over to see Wanda and Crazy Dan. "One needs a full stomach to deal sensitively with the mystical," explained Myrtle to Miles as a waitress handed her a plate with a pimento cheese-covered hotdog alongside a generous helping of chili cheese fries.

Miles looked a bit queasy as he observed Myrtle. "I don't honestly know how you've reached your advanced years while maintaining a diet that includes decades of food from Bo's Diner." He had searched the laminated menu for something a little healthier and had come up with a bowl of chicken noodle soup. The waitress put it in front of him with an apologetic air. "You sure this is what you want, hon?" Her eyes gazed in concern at him through heavily mascara-coated lashes. He nodded, but looked longingly across the room at another diner's blue plate special.

"That talk with Rose was uncomfortable, wasn't it?" Myrtle made a face. "I might have to avoid attending book club in the near future."

"Wasn't that part of your general plan anyway? Avoiding book club at all costs?" Miles took an unenthusiastic sip of his soup. It was apparently better than he expected, and he took another sip immediately afterward.

"It's one way that I ensure having a good week," admitted Myrtle. "But now with Rose freezing me out, it's going to seem even more unattractive than usual."

"She acted pretty appalled that you thought she had something to do with a murder."

Myrtle finished up her hotdog and sized up her chili cheese fries. She decided they would be better attacked with a knife and fork. She dug into them with gusto. "You've gotten right to the heart of it, Miles, as usual."

Miles frowned at her. "The heart of it?"

"When you said *acted*. She *acted* appalled that I thought she had something to do with Naomi's murder. Like she's never heard it even hinted that she could somehow be involved. When you know that Red Clover and Detective Lieutenant Perkins with the state police have been over there asking her questions."

Miles said, "Oh. Well, we all like to maintain these little fictions about ourselves, don't we? It helps get through the day. Maybe Rose didn't want to admit to company that she was a suspect in a murder investigation. Or maybe Red and Perkins are treading really lightly and hoping Rose will just shoot herself in the foot by giving out more information than she planned on giving." He appeared to be nearly finished with the bowl of chicken noodle soup. "It might have been a good tactic for you to take, Myrtle. You know...instead of informing her that she didn't follow her mom's rule of 'if you don't have anything nice to say.'"

"That just popped out of my mouth," muttered Myrtle. "Besides, I've always subscribed to a variation of that axiom."

"Which is?"

"If you don't have anything nice to say, come sit down next to me." Myrtle polished off her chili cheese fries.

The waitress came by with perfect timing. "Want some key lime pie, sweetie?" She took away the empty plate.

"Why not?"

Miles said, "I bow down to your superior arteries, Myrtle. You'd have to take me out of Bo's Diner on a stretcher if I had all the stuff you've eaten today."

"Pooh. Whatever. It just takes practice, that's all," said Myrtle with imperfect logic. She took a big sip of iced tea. "I don't honestly know if Rose is our best suspect anymore."

Miles blinked at her owlishly from behind his rimless spectacles. "Why on earth not? I thought you'd just established that she lied to us, that she hosted a murder in her own living room, and that she knew enough about horticulture to pull off such a feat."

Myrtle waved a hand impatiently at him. "Yes, yes, that's all true. But did you catch what she was saying at the end there?"

"About holding your tongue if you don't have something nice to say? Of course I caught it—we were *just* talking about how you turned it all back around on her." Miles looked sadly at the empty bottom of his soup bowl as it was whisked away by their waitress.

"But did you catch the *significance* of what she was saying? That she knew something. Something about the murder. And she had no plans of sharing this information." Myrtle beamed at her key lime pie as it was placed in front of her.

"Couldn't she have just been using that as a cover-up? To deflect attention away from herself?" asked Miles.

"I don't want to give Rose credit for being that clever. For all her aristocratic airs and her primness, I don't believe she's the sharpest tool in the shed." Myrtle closed her eyes briefly in bliss as she took a mouthful of the pie.

"What gives you that impression?" Miles frowned.

"I taught her," said Myrtle simply. "And I remember her grades and the fact she never once finished her homework. Disgraceful. I had to call her mama—the one with all the rules. I do believe that's why Rose is still giving me such a hard time."

Miles was dismayed to find that his stomach was starting to rumble just watching Myrtle's key lime pie disappear. "Want something else to eat, sugar?" suggested the waitress, who seemed to have her finger on the pulse of everyone at the diner.

"No, I think we're finished," said Miles firmly. "Ready to head over to see Wanda, Myrtle?"

Myrtle raised her eyebrows at him but didn't say a word.

Wanda, usually called Wander by her brother, Crazy Dan, lived in a hubcap-covered hut off the side of the old highway that served as both a business and a home for the two. The business was the sort that sold live bait, hubcaps, peanuts, and psychic prophecy. Myrtle had never seen any evidence of any business actually transpiring there. Miles had made the shocking and unwelcome discovery that he was a cousin of Wanda and Crazy

Dan's and had been even more reluctant to go there with Myrtle since then. His hands gripped the steering wheel as if he were trying to force himself not to turn the car around and head back home.

Miles frowned. "Did you tell Wanda we were coming?"

"How precisely would I have done that? Mental telepathy? They don't have phones you know."

Miles said slowly, "Then how did she know?"

Myrtle squinted through the windshield. Sure enough, Wanda was sitting in a disreputable-looking plastic chair in the dusty yard. A wobbly table was next to her with three glasses full of a dark substance, and she had two other plastic chairs of varying styles and colors next to her. When Miles pulled his sedan up to park, Wanda lifted her glass in a salute.

"She knew because she's psychic, Miles. That's what I keep telling you. It's the whole point we're here, for heaven's sake. Do pay attention." Myrtle grabbed her cane and pushed open the passenger side door with gusto.

"I know you keep telling me that," muttered Miles, "it's just that I haven't believed it."

"Hi Wanda," called out Myrtle, thumping with her cane through the dusty red dirt as she made her way over to the seating area that Wanda had set up for them. She and Miles sat gingerly down in the precariously unsteady chairs and Wanda smiled at them in greeting, revealing quite a few missing teeth.

"Have a drink," Wanda croaked in her cigarette-ruined voice.

Miles looked suspiciously at the glass. "I'm not thirsty," he said. But apparently a bit of dust had lodged in his throat and he immediately commenced into a coughing fit.

Myrtle rolled her eyes and picked up her glass. She had her own doubts about the glass and its contents, but only gave a moment's hesitation.

"It's clean," said Wanda.

"And the stuff in the glass?" asked Miles, still coughing convulsively.

"Tea."

Miles and Myrtle took cautious sips from the glasses. The tea seemed all right and the glasses did appear clean. This was miraculous, considering the rest of the house.

"Y'all should trust me," said Wanda reproachfully.

"We do," said Myrtle quickly.

Wanda shook her head. "Don't. Never do. You put me down like Red puts you down." Wanda made a spiraling gesture with a bony, nicotine-stained hand to simulate something that resembled the path of a crashing airplane.

"Well, I hardly think *that's* true. Otherwise, why would I have taken the trouble to come all the way out here to talk to you? Red won't even cross the street to get my opinion," said Myrtle, making a face. Then she said in a quiet voice, "Wanda, I promise you that I value your opinion. Sometimes, you're the only person who seems to make any sense at all."

A momentary pleased smile lit up Wanda's lean face. And then she was all business. "You want a clue," said Wanda, cutting to the chase as usual.

"Have you got one for me?"

"Yer in danger," said Wanda grimly.

Miles gave Myrtle a meaningful look. Every single time Myrtle had made the pilgrimage to Wanda's shack, she was told that she was in mortal danger. It had become something of a joke between them.

"All right, yes, I've got that," said Myrtle tightly. "Anything else, though?"

Wanda tilted her face up to the weak rays of the sun filtering through the pine trees as if collecting psychic wisdom. She hoarsely grated, "The key is in the van."

Myrtle and Miles stared blankly at her.

Wanda lowered her face and looked back at them. "That is all."

"The key is in the van," murmured Miles.

"What on earth kind of a clue is that, Wanda? It doesn't make any sense." Myrtle glared at the woman perched in the rickety plastic chair.

Wanda shrugged a skeletal shoulder. "The key is in the van."

"All right," said Myrtle. "Well, I guess all will become clear in some huge, clarifying moment of grace at some point in the near future. I suppose we should go now. Thanks for the drinks." She rummaged around in her gigantic pocketbook for some money, but Miles beat her to it, surprising her by handing his cousin what looked to be several twenties.

"Take care," said Miles gruffly. He walked abruptly off to the car, leaving Myrtle to stare at his back in amazement.

"Yer cat is okay, too," said Wanda. "Don't worry about the cat."

Myrtle swung around to gape at Wanda again. "You know about Pasha? Did you see my flyers out?"

Wanda gave her a scornful look. "Hasn't been to town. Cars is broke."

Myrtle glanced around the dusty yard to confirm that, indeed, all of the corroded vehicles on the premises appeared to be up on cement blocks.

"She's okay?" Myrtle asked her intently.

"She's laying low until them dogs behaves themselves," said Wanda, nodding. "She's okay. She's smart."

Wanda walked with Myrtle to Miles's car. "Watch it. Root," she warned Myrtle at one point, helping Myrtle navigate around a pine tree root that was particularly treacherous. Myrtle put her cane in Miles's backseat, and then climbed into the passenger side.

Miles started the engine and they were about to drive away when Wanda started banging on the side of the car. Myrtle put down her window and Wanda said hoarsely, "Fergot. Had something fer you." The woman patted at her pockets, and then pulled something out, stretching it out to Myrtle in a bony hand. "A gift."

Miles stared at the item silently. Myrtle cleared her throat and said, "Thank you, Wanda. Very much."

Miles backed the car up and Wanda called after them, "The key is in the van!"

As they drove off, Miles said dryly, "I'm glad I never had to endure family Christmases with her, if that's her idea of a gift."

They both stared at the container of pepper spray in Myrtle's lap. Myrtle gave it a small pat. "Don't you see, though? Wanda is looking out for me. She clearly thinks this is something I might need."

"No surprise there. After all, she's always giving you those dire prophesies. It's a wonder she hasn't given you a weapon before now." Miles carefully took a curve on the rural road.

"She told me Pasha was all right," said Myrtle softly.

"Trying to make you feel better, I guess. Nice of her."

"But how did she *know* about Pasha?" persisted Myrtle.

"Maybe Pasha came for a visit," said Miles with a shrug.

Myrtle smiled. Miles was so pragmatic that she knew he could never officially accept that Wanda was gifted in any way.

"It was kind of you to give her money," said Myrtle, looking sideways at Miles.

Miles flushed and grew a bit flustered. "Well, you know. Family connection and all. She's such a sad thing. I feel bad."

Myrtle looked at him in surprise. "Sad? No. I think Wanda is okay. But it was still nice of you."

They drove back in thoughtful quiet for the rest of the trip.

Chapter Eight

Miles pulled up into Myrtle's driveway. "Thanks for the ride, Miles. And for going with me this morning to see Rose."

Miles was carefully backing out when he saw that Myrtle was not walking to her front door at all, but was heading down the sidewalk, leaning fairly heavily on her cane. "Aren't you done for today? I thought it was time for your soap?"

Myrtle grinned at him. "You *know* it's time for my soap. That's because you're hooked on it, too. I'm fine on my own, Miles. You should go ahead and fix yourself a grilled cheese and sit down in front of *Tomorrow's Promise* for a while."

Miles closed his eyes briefly as if praying for patience. Then he pushed open the passenger side door. "Hop on in."

"But you were planning on going back home!"

"I guess I'll end up going back home just a little later than I'd planned. Besides, sidekicks are supposed to go along *with* the sleuths—that's the whole point of being a sidekick. So I'll go along with you to...?" Miles gave Myrtle an expectant look.

"To Maxine Tristan's house," supplied Myrtle.

"To Maxine's house," said Miles. He sighed. "Even though Maxine makes me a bit flustered." He took off his glasses and wiped the lenses on his shirt as if even thinking about the woman was making him rattled.

Myrtle sat back down in the passenger seat with a bit of a thump. Her knees were starting to give her some complaints this afternoon, although she'd never admit it to Miles. He continued backing up, giving Red a brief wave as he and Myrtle headed back out again.

Myrtle resisted the urge to stick her tongue out at Red. She knew he was the one behind Miles's courteous chauffeuring. Red must have come home for lunch and that was the second time he'd given Miles that wave of approval and thanks. Most irritating. And now Myrtle was feeling in a rather grouchy mood, when she hadn't been before. "We've spent all day together," groused Myrtle. "People will say we're having a love affair."

Miles raised his eyebrows at her. "Since when do you mind what people say?"

"Well, you know. Small town and all of that. And I do mind what people say. I absolutely despise it when people call me *sweetie* and *young lady*. Especially *young lady* in that jaunty kind of tone. Makes me want to smack them."

Myrtle continued fuming in the passenger seat and Miles wisely stayed silent until she got it out of her system. When Myrtle appeared to be simmering down a bit, Miles cautiously said, "Remind me again about Maxine? I mean...remind me why she's a suspect. What's her motive, again?"

"Well, I was tipped off to Maxine when she was positively grinning when Naomi's death was announced at book club. It wasn't merely inappropriate—it was quite telling. Lena Fowler also brought up Maxine. She wouldn't tell me much, but she mentioned that Maxine saw Naomi as competition of some kind. I guess Maxine must have thought that Naomi was after her boyfriend—something like that! That does seem to be Naomi's usual modus operandi. But Maxine doesn't seem like the kind of woman men leave. I mean, she's quite attractive," said Myrtle.

Miles grew flustered again. Really, this was going to be most amusing if Miles kept getting discombobulated whenever Maxine or Maxine's appearance was brought up. He must have quite a crush.

They arrived at a small white house with a bit of gingerbread trim on the sides and a front porch just large enough to hold three rocking chairs.

"It almost looks as if she knew we were coming. Look, three chairs, Miles," said Myrtle.

"Is she psychic, too?" asked Miles in a grouchy tone.

Maxine didn't seem to have any otherworldly talents as far as Myrtle could tell. She seemed, in fact, very focused on making the most of her physical talents. Maxine was an attractive woman in a very obvious way. She greeted them with delight, as if she wanted nothing more for the afternoon than to entertain an extremely elderly woman and her widower companion. She had on a rather tight purple top and a rather short black skirt and wore espadrilles and a lot of eye makeup.

"You're staring at her," said Myrtle, glaring at Miles as Maxine hurried inside to get them some lemonade.

"I'm trying not to," said Miles in a strained voice. "But Maxine always wears very tight garments. It's very difficult to avoid staring."

"Here we are," sang out Maxine as she joined them again on the porch. She set down a tray with lemonade for the three of them on a small table and then distributed the glasses. Myrtle took a sip and raised her eyebrows. Homemade lemonade.

"I'm delighted to see y'all today, but of course I know you must be here on a mission," said Maxine, getting right to the point. Perhaps she *did* have something to do after they left this afternoon. "What might it be? A message about next month's selection for book club? A rescheduled garden club meeting? Fundraising for impoverished Eastern European children?" Maxine gave a perfect smile with her perfectly lipsticked mouth and her perfectly gleaming teeth.

Miles cleared his throat. "Well, actually–" He began hoarsely.

"Actually," Myrtle stepped in smoothly, "Miles is helping me hand out flyers."

Myrtle was all set to go into her spiel about Pasha, what she looked like, and the circumstances of her mysterious disappearance when Maxine nodded with complete understanding.

"That's right," she said with total recall, "at the book club meeting you mentioned that you'd lost your cat. A black cat. Pasha. There was a scuffle involving those mongrel dogs, right? You haven't found her yet?"

Myrtle gaped at Maxine in amazement. Here was apparently the one person at book club who had actually been paying attention to Myrtle. And she could even remember all the small details, including the cat's name.

Maxine smiled at her. "Are these the flyers you're putting out?" She held out a well-manicured hand to take one from Myrtle. Myrtle handed one to her, wordlessly. She could see a tiny tattoo on Maxine's shoulder that briefly came into view before her purple top covered it again.

Maxine studied the flyer. "All right. Now that I know Miss Pasha's face, I'll be on the lookout for her. Don't worry about her. I remember I lost a cat once...years and years ago. Buttons was gone for two months. I'd given up hope that she was coming back—I'd searched and searched so...you know. I figured the poor creature had gotten run over by a car or another animal or something. Grieved a bit. Cried a while. I was in recovery mode, thinking about getting another pet. Then one day, up comes Buttons on the front porch, bold as brass. Acting as if she'd only been away for an afternoon instead of a couple of months." Maxine lit up a cigarette and gave a reflective puff. "Darned cat."

Myrtle had never been a fan of cigarettes and it was that fact that she attributed to helping her live to her advanced age. She tried inconspicuously to push her chair backward to escape the toxic blue fumes that seemed to be wafting her way.

The perceptive Maxine noticed. She grimaced. "Sorry about that." She turned her head, took a few puffs, and then stubbed out the cigarette, sticking it in her shorts pocket. "Nasty habit."

Myrtle wasn't sure how to get the topic back to murder and away from cats without being completely obvious. And was amazed when Miles made the segue for her.

"It's been an exciting week all right," said Miles a bit gruffly. "Missing cat. A campaign to find said missing cat. And, of course—Naomi's death."

Maxine gave him a toothy grin. "Well, I'm glad you said it was an *exciting* week and not a *sad* one. Because Naomi Pelter's death was certainly a highlight for me."

Myrtle and Miles just gaped at her. Surely, she hadn't intended to say such a thing out loud.

"Actually, I should amend that. Naomi Pelter's *murder* was a highlight." Maxine took a sip of her lemonade and rocked reflectively in the rocker for a moment. Then she turned to look at Myrtle and Miles. "Have I scandalized you?"

Myrtle cleared her throat. "Your honesty is refreshing. Most people try not to speak ill of the dead."

"Most people are idiots," said Maxine with a shrug. "I didn't particularly like Naomi and that hasn't changed since her death. She tended to chase after men I'd become involved with." She gave Miles a rather salacious wink and he turned bright red.

"You know that the police are calling it murder," said Myrtle.

"Word gets around," said Maxine.

"The police haven't asked you any questions?" asked Myrtle.

"No."

Myrtle felt smug. She was one-step ahead of Red and the state police. "Have you thought about who might have killed her?"

"So that I can throw them a party?" asked Maxine archly. "I haven't really thought it out, no. Although, if I had to name names, Rose Mayfield would come up pretty fast. She's the obvious candidate, right?"

"Can you come up with a less-obvious candidate?"

Maxine furrowed her brow and put both manicured hands on the sides of her head as if pushing out the thoughts. Then she snapped her fingers. "Claudia Brown," she said. She rolled her eyes. "Poor, poor Claudia."

"When I visited Claudia...about Pasha, you know...she mentioned that she liked Naomi," said Myrtle.

Maxine was starting to look bored. "As I said, most people are idiots. If someone dies, the idiots suddenly have to pretend they were best friends with victim, when they weren't."

Miles appeared to have recovered from his last flustering. "Why do you call Claudia poor?"

"She's very simple. And she is so proud of being able to sing well—her one talent, you know. When Naomi identified things that were important to people, she decided to steal them away. That's the kind of person she was. She noticed that Claudia loved being the soloist at the church and got many compliments and attention that way. Next thing you know, Naomi is heading off to church and is lead soloist." Maxine absently rubbed the red lipstick mark that was now on her lemonade glass.

"So you're not surprised at all that Naomi was murdered," said Myrtle.

"Only that it didn't happen earlier," said Maxine stoutly. "Finished with your lemonade?" she asked in a more pleasant tone.

"I think I know why Maxine flusters you so much, Miles. She's a real piece of work." Myrtle and Miles were back in Miles's car and heading back home.

"She's a very brazen young woman," said Miles, still looking a little ruddy.

"She was flirting with you." Myrtle pursed her lips. It might possibly be considered condescending for a lovely young woman to flirt with a gentleman Miles's age and she hated condescension. If it wasn't condescension, it was certainly impertinence.

"I believe it's what comes naturally to her. I think she may flirt with anyone. I think it's her normal way of interacting with people," said Miles in a mild voice.

They pulled up into Myrtle's driveway. "Well, thanks for driving me here and yonder today. You even missed your soap."

Miles winced. "Please don't keep saying that. I really don't want people to think I'm a regular soap opera viewer."

Myrtle said, "Why don't you come in and watch it with me? I've got ice cream. We can have chocolate ice cream with chocolate syrup. I tape the show and I know you don't. We can find out if Cheryl and Justin ever escaped from that mad bomber. And if Kayla got away from the cult."

Miles sighed. "The fact that those are examples of actual storylines makes me wonder again why I'm watching the show. But the ice cream does sound really good."

"Sometimes you have to have bubble gum for the brain," said Myrtle. "Gives me an opportunity to rest my mind a little while."

"Okay," said Miles. "Although don't get mad if I drift off during the show. I'm feeling pretty tired out. I'm not like you,

you know. You have more energy than a two-year-old on caffeine."

He followed Myrtle in and helped her fix the bowls of ice cream. They brought them into Myrtle's small living room and she messed with a couple of remotes for a few minutes until a menu came up. She grunted, looking at the list of shows. "Where's *Tomorrow's Promise*?"

"Didn't it tape?"

"I can't find it on the list! What on earth?" Myrtle kept scrolling up and down on the list of taped shows. "What's wrong with this thing?"

"Flip over to live TV and see what's on that station," said Miles. "Maybe the show got preempted for some reason."

Myrtle muttered under her breath, fumbling with the remotes again until she pulled up the station that *Tomorrow's Promise* ordinarily showed on. "Tennis! For heaven's sake. Tennis is on."

"I rather like tennis," said Miles in a mild tone. He took a big bite of his chocolate ice cream with chocolate syrup.

"I only watch tennis when it airs on Sundays," said Myrtle stoutly. "Why is it coming on during the week in the afternoon?"

"It's a tournament," said Miles. "It's not as if we missed anything. The show didn't come on today. So when it's back on tomorrow, they'll pick up where they left off."

"Yes, thank you, I understand the way preempted shows work," groused Myrtle. "I'm just annoyed that a sporting event is messing up my plans."

"We could watch tennis," suggested Miles, "since you don't mind watching it either. This Russian woman who is playing now is supposed to be very good."

"No, because now I'm annoyed at the tennis game for bumping off my show," said Myrtle. She fumed for a moment, staring at her melting ice cream. "Now I feel restless again. Maybe I should go put out more flyers for Pasha."

"Myrtle! Haven't you done enough today? Besides, you've covered the area, and talked to enough suspects for one day, too."

"I don't want to talk to more suspects today," said Myrtle. "But putting out more flyers makes sense."

"It doesn't, actually," said Miles in a patient voice that set Myrtle's teeth on edge. "I've been reading up on data about missing cats. One article I read said that cats could become quite disoriented when they're in even slightly unfamiliar territory...particularly if they were driven out of their usual stomping grounds by a catfight or by being chased by a dog. They hide, apparently. Even if they're very close by, they might be too scared to come out and are worried about where they are."

Myrtle was in a mood where hearing logic annoyed her. And she was already put out with the change of plans for the rest of the afternoon and the fact that it didn't involve her soap opera. And maybe the busy day had taken more out of her than she'd previously suspected. There was also the fact that, despite the positive message Wanda had given her, she was worried sick over that cat. Being worried sick wasn't particularly good for Myrtle, either. So it was in an unfortunate icy tone that she asserted, "You're just saying that because you think Pasha isn't coming back home to me. You're trying to let me down easily. You think she's been run over by a car or something. Or that she's sick or injured and crawled off into the woods to die." These were her worst fears and something that she hadn't allowed herself to voice earlier.

Miles glanced away briefly. "I'm only saying–" he started out, stiffly.

"You don't even *like* Pasha," shot back Myrtle in a furious voice.

Miles just blinked at her, his eyes stunned behind the rimless glasses, a bit of chocolate on the corner of his mouth. Then a hurt expression flickered across his face and he carefully took his empty ice cream bowl into the kitchen, rinsed it, and put it into the dishwasher.

"We can talk more about this after we've calmed down," he said quietly. He didn't seem as if he needed to calm down. He picked up his keys and left.

Chapter Nine

The unusual quarrel with Miles was the catalyst that set Myrtle's night into a downward spiral. She slept restlessly that night and was plagued with insomnia at two-thirty in the morning. She'd had to squash her first instinct, which was to go over to Miles for their milk and cookies.

Myrtle decided to channel her insomnia and restlessness into something more productive. She started a load of laundry, emptied her dishwasher, and then sat down at her computer to write the news story about the mushroom poisoning. She wrote about Naomi and her involvement in both book club and garden club. She mentioned that the garden club had brought in a special speaker from the county extension office who had talked at great length about poisonous mushrooms, as well as other garden problems. Without coming right out and making the connection, since it was a news story, she wrote that not long after that meeting, Naomi had been poisoned by a Destroying Angel mushroom.

Myrtle read over the story carefully, tweaking her word choice and ensuring the article was as factual as she could make it. Then she opened up another document and wrote her regular, helpful hints column. She had several decent things to put in there this time...it really all depended on what people emailed over to her. A couple of times she's unapologetically made up tips, not having any material. It kept her creativity alive, she'd decided. But this time she had a tip for putting a dry towel in with a wet load in the dryer to speed up the drying process. And a tip for using old milk containers as watering cans by poking holes into the plastic cap.

Myrtle ended her tip column with an appeal to the public to keep an eye out for Pasha.

She hopefully looked outside her front window to see if her newspaper had come—at this point, it was four o'clock in the morning. It hadn't, but it arrived thirty minutes later with a skidding sound on her front walk. Myrtle fetched it, and quickly finished the crossword puzzle. Then she read over the tips column and the news story one more time and emailed them to her editor, Sloan.

Myrtle was walking into her kitchen for a refill of coffee when her computer made a chiming sound to let her know she'd gotten an email. She frowned and headed back over to the desktop.

There was an immediate response from Sloan there. She was amazed that he woke up this early. The email said: *I'm sorry, Miss Myrtle, but I can't run this story. Thanks for the tip column, though, and good luck with the missing cat. It's always a good idea to add a bit of human interest to a column—great job.*

Myrtle hadn't been trying to add human interest to the column. She'd just wanted to get her cat back. And it was extremely annoying about the news story. Red continued shutting her down at every turn. It was turning out to be a most unsatisfactory day already...and it was only five a.m.

It was after breakfast when things became worse.

Myrtle's phone rang at eight-thirty and she frowned at the wall phone. Phone calls before nine o'clock in the morning were tacky. She walked over and picked up. "Hello?" she asked.

A nasal and insistent voice said, "Is this Myrtle Clover?"

"Tell me who this is, first," said Myrtle impatiently. "You're the one making the call."

"This is Nan, a representative from Greener Pastures Retirement Home. Is this Myrtle Clover?"

"Yes it is," said Myrtle guardedly.

"We understand that you want to be placed on the waiting list for Greener Pastures," said the woman in a rather pompous tone.

Myrtle spluttered, "That I *want* to be on the waiting list? Pardon me?"

The voice continued, nasally. "We don't take every applicant to Greener Pastures. Some are simply not suited. You will need to come in and demonstrate that you're able enough to be a resident at our facility. And we'll want you to take our tour so that you can get a better sense of the kind of residence we provide."

Myrtle was struck speechless. Then she rallied enough to say in a dangerous growl, "*You* interview *me*?"

"That is the procedure."

Myrtle said in a voice so angry it shook, "I can assure you, that if I get to that point of sheer desperation where I need to be shipped off to a retirement home, *I* will be the one interviewing *you*. And I doubt very much that you'll measure up. I do *not* want to be on your waiting list. I've no intention of residing at your facility."

"We received a phone call," droned the woman.

"Only because my son is being obstreperous." And Myrtle slammed down the phone, breathing hard. Her eyes narrowed with determination. The only possible response to this foolishness was to pull her entire ceramic gnome collection out into her front yard. There was no more effective means of displaying her displeasure with Red than to force him to endure a vista of gnomes when he gazed out his front windows.

Myrtle's mind worked overtime as she lugged out the gnomes, positioning them as close to the road as she could. Surely, it was time for things to start looking up. A fight with Miles? A rejected article for the newspaper? A recruitment call from the retirement home? And all of this on top of her missing cat. Myrtle decided she needed to get out of the house and focus on the case. Sitting around the house worrying about stuff that was out of her control was for ninnies.

But where was she? What did she need to do next? Talking to Miles was always good to help her figure out a clear path. Now she'd have to figure out her next step on her own and she frowned as she focused. She'd talked with everyone once. But where did she need to follow up?

Rose was the obvious suspect. But something made her feel uneasy about Rose and she couldn't put her finger on it. Was it the fact that she alluded that she knew someone who had a grudge against Naomi? Did she know more than she was letting on? Or did Myrtle feel uneasy simply because Rose held some latent, or not-so-latent, animosity against her?

Rose would be her first visit today. Her manner bothered her, if nothing else. Maybe she could catch Rose off-guard today and get her to be more forthcoming. When she'd talked with her yesterday, Myrtle felt as if she didn't do a good job really pushing her for information. She'd let Rose push her away a bit. Today, she might push more on the topic of poisonous mushrooms. Then she could try to gauge her reaction.

Thinking about garden club made Myrtle take a peek into her backyard. Dry as a bone, as she'd figured. She'd run the sprinkler in the front yard a couple of days ago, but neglected to water the back. She attached the sprinkler to the hose, turned the spigot on, shook the water from the leaking connection off her hand, and then hurried back inside.

Myrtle finished getting ready and found her cane. She was glad that all the activity from the day before hadn't made her sore today because it looked as if she was going to be doing some walking.

As she stepped outside, she automatically looked for Pasha. But all she saw was crabgrass...and Erma driving off, giving a toot of her horn and a wave to Myrtle as she left. Myrtle decided to take this opportunity to fling more of that homemade weed killer into Erma's front yard, close to the border of Myrtle's yard. A natural boundary to keep the stuff from creeping over. Feeling pleased for the first time that day, Myrtle put the container back in the house, locked the door behind her, and headed over to Rose's house.

It seemed unusually quiet on Rose's street this morning. Surely, everyone must be awake. It wasn't as if it were early. Myrtle double-checked her watch to make sure. No, it was a perfectly reasonable ten o'clock. But there was no one walking down the street, no one doing yard work. And, of course, Naomi was dead—no activity at her house at all.

Myrtle walked up Rose's front walk and to the front door. She rapped on the door and waited for an answer. Nothing. She rang the doorbell—surely, Rose was up. Her car was in the driveway, so she should be home. It seemed rather late in the morning for Rose to be taking a shower or some such thing...she was an early bird. No answer. Myrtle rang it again, and then rapped on the front door again—still no answer.

Then Myrtle tried the door handle and found that it turned and the door opened. Was Rose the kind of person who left her door unlocked all the time? She knew Bradley was a small town, but Red had always drilled into Myrtle's head that small towns had bad guys, too. Myrtle cautiously stuck her head in through the front door. "Yoo-hoo! Rose! It's Myrtle Clover."

She listened for an answer, but heard none.

Myrtle paused for a moment, then opened the door farther and said in a louder voice, "Rose? It's Myrtle Clover. Can I come in for a few minutes?"

Nothing.

Myrtle suddenly reached into her tremendous purse and fumbled inside until her fingers closed on a small object. She pulled out the pepper spray that Wanda had given her and proceeded into the quiet house.

Myrtle gripped her cane tightly in her hand as she walked. "Rose?"

She walked across the hardwood floor and into the living room...and swayed just a bit as she saw a figure on the floor in nearly the same spot as Naomi Pelter's body had lain. It was Rose Mayfield, dead in a pool of blood, with a fireplace poker lying next to her.

Myrtle's head swam as she surveyed the scene in front of her. She glanced quickly around her with a sharp eye, but saw no sign that the killer was still here. The door had been unlocked—it seemed likely that Rose knew her murderer and had let him in. Perhaps he left by the same route.

She needed to call Red. Myrtle opened up her purse, sticking the pepper spray back inside, and reached for her cell phone. Then she paused. Red was going to shut her down, but good. Was there anything, anything at all that she could see quickly before he got here?

Myrtle dialed Red's number slowly, glancing around her. No signs of a struggle that she could see. Everything was in the right place, except for the fireplace poker. The only injury that Myrtle spotted was the gash on the back of Rose's head...and Rose was lying face down, which suggested to Myrtle that she'd been hit from behind. Which suggested something else—that Rose felt comfortable enough to turn her back on her attacker.

Red picked up on the fourth ring. "Mama? Is everything okay? I was going to call you later to see if you wanted me to take you to the store."

"The store? Maybe. I don't know. Listen, Red, I'm in Rose Mayfield's house—"

"*What*?" Red's voice was loud enough for Myrtle to pull the phone away from her head.

"Calm down, Red. Rose and I have been dealing with some...garden club business. Anyway ..."

"Since when have you become a gardening fanatic? Last I saw, Elaine had to practically drag you to one of the meetings," said Red in a grumpy voice.

"Since Erma Sherman has been driving me crazy by allowing her nasty crabgrass to creep over into my yard," said Myrtle with a sniff. "Now *listen*. For once." Red stopped talking and Myrtle took a deep breath. "I came over to Rose's house and her door was unlocked. I walked inside and found that she's...well...she's dead."

"*What?*"

Red was starting to sound like a broken record. Or perhaps he was getting hard of hearing. He *was* in his forties, after all. She loudly repeated, "Rose Mayfield is dead! In her living room. With a fireplace poker. You might want to see about it."

Myrtle hung up the phone as Red continued spluttering. She continued looking around the room, standing very still so as not to disturb anything.

And she found that Rose kept her house very tidy. Disappointingly tidy. As a matter of fact, there really weren't even any clues to Rose's personality here in the room. No photographs of family. No books lying around.

The only thing anywhere in the room was a spiral-bound crossword puzzle book. As a fellow crossword aficionado, Myrtle walked closer to get a look at the book, stooping down to see it without touching it.

Rose was apparently the kind of crossword puzzle solver who liked to pen firm answers to the crossword clues in ink. She even jotted down ideas for clues in the margins of the book in pencil until she was sure that the possibility would fit. Then she appeared to erase the penciled-in idea. This alone spoke to her personality. But there was something even more interesting on the page.

Rose had written down *seating arrangement?* in the margin. But, as Myrtle scanned the puzzle, she couldn't see a potential clue that fit the answer—or a spot on the puzzle that the answer would fit in. As a matter of fact, Myrtle didn't think that Rose had jotted that down in conjunction with the puzzle at all. She'd written it in ink, too, as if she were too distracted to use her usual method of penciling something in.

Suddenly, she heard a bumping noise from the direction of the kitchen. She straightened up after having been stooped over the end table and stuck her hand in her purse, grabbing her pepper spray. Was this person coming after her?

Chapter Ten

Myrtle heard the kitchen door swiftly slam behind whoever was rapidly leaving. She hurried to the window, but saw nothing. There were woods bordering that side of the house (more of Rose's precious trees) and the intruder had taken advantage of their cover to escape.

So Rose must have just been murdered. Myrtle shuddered at the thought that she could have walked in on a murder in progress if she'd arrived moments earlier. She jumped as she heard the sound of a door again and then realized it was Red coming at last.

Red called out, an anxious sharpness to his voice, "Mama? Mama, where are you?"

"I'm in the living room, Red. Right here."

Red hurried in, his face relaxing a little when he saw she was all right, but then tensing up again when he saw the slumped figure on the floor. "What in the Sam Hill is going on here? Two murders in Rose Mayfield's house in the last week?" He pulled out a handkerchief and quickly swabbed his forehead. Then he placed a quick, terse phone call to the State Bureau of Investigations (SBI), which was the North Carolina State Police. "What were you doing here again?"

Myrtle hesitated. After receiving the phone call from Greener Pastures that morning, she wasn't exactly in a sharing, cooperative type of mood. Red would be furious if he thought she was poking around in the murder still. She thought she might just test his detective skills a little and see if he or the state police noticed the crossword puzzle book. Myrtle had a feeling they might overlook the clue—the *real* clue.

So, instead, she said firmly, "I'd asked Rose to be on the lookout for Pasha. I gave her a flyer and all. I was following up with her to see whether she'd spotted her. Rose spends a lot of time outside, gardening."

Red raised his eyebrows, glancing around. "Doesn't look like Rose paid all that much attention to the flyer. I don't see it lying around or posted on her French doors or anything."

Myrtle snapped, "Maybe she's got it on her fridge. Who knows? Maybe she has a photographic memory and simply stared at Pasha's picture and then tossed the paper. Who cares what *I* was doing here, anyway? I didn't kill Rose. But I surprised the person who did."

Red drew in a gasping breath. "You did? You saw him?"

"No, I didn't see him, I *surprised* him. When he heard me calling out for Rose when I opened the door, he hid in the kitchen. I heard him run out a few minutes later. I guess he must have run into the woods," said Myrtle.

"Seems likely," said Red. His lips were pulled down into a ferocious frown.

"I'm sure no one saw a fleeing suspect, either," said Myrtle. "No one sees anything in this town!" She glared at Rose's body.

"Now, it's hardly Rose's fault that she was too dead to witness the killer's getaway," said Red with a roll of his eyes. "I told you to keep out of all this, if you remember. Don't think I'm buying the story about the cat. I have a terrible feeling this is all going to end poorly if you don't butt out, Mama. This person means business. He might even have seen you through the kitchen door or a reflection or something. Might have recognized your voice."

Myrtle guiltily recalled that she'd identified herself as she'd entered Rose's house. "So this murderer might have seen you snooping and is deciding that you're next, Mama."

"I wasn't snooping!" Myrtle drew back as if she'd been stung, her face flushing with the lie.

"Regardless, you're probably in danger. Why don't you just do something fun to distract yourself? Go to Bo's Diner with Miles or something."

Myrtle looked away and Red said slowly, "Oh no. You haven't offended Miles, have you?"

"He offends *me*!" Myrtle clenched her hand tightly over the hook of her cane. "And so do you! What on earth was that phone call this morning about?"

Red genuinely looked puzzled. "Phone call? I didn't make a phone call this morning."

"From Greener Pastures. They called me and said I had to be interviewed by them to see if I were suitable or some such nonsense."

Red sighed. "They called you? Well, that's irritating."

His mother continued to glare at him and Red said quickly, "Mama, is this really the right time and place to have an argument about this? Standing over a dead woman?"

He could see Myrtle wasn't letting him off the hook, though. He said, "I knew something was up when I saw those blasted gnomes in your yard. Yes, I put you on the waiting list. It's the kind of waiting list where you can wait for until you need them. If they call and tell you there's an opening, we can tell them no and then they put you back on the waiting list again. See? The place does fill up, Mama. There might come a time when you need them and *they're* not available."

"I will *not* need them."

"You might like Greener Pastures if you took a real tour of the place," said Red.

"I've been there a million times! Visiting my poor, pitiful friends who ended up in that dive."

Red closed his eyes. "But it wasn't a tour. And the people you were visiting probably weren't making it sound as great as it is." He was about to continue on this line of thought when his phone rang again. "Okay, we're done here, Mama. I need to get you out of here—the state police are on their way." He walked Myrtle safely outside and then walked back in to wait for the state police.

Red's mulishness on the subject of Greener Pastures merely reinforced Myrtle's decision not to share her crossword puzzle findings with either him or the state police. If Red was so smart and knew best, then let him figure out that the clue in the margin wasn't related to the puzzle at all.

Besides, Myrtle didn't know exactly what it meant, herself. But, at least it had given her a line of inquiry. What seating arrangements was Rose talking about? Did it have something to do with book club? Myrtle furrowed her brow. No, it couldn't have. There were never any seating arrangements at book club. It must be that garden club luncheon that she didn't attend. Had someone been sitting in the wrong place? Had someone rearranged the place cards, perhaps? Perhaps Rose had seen the person do it. Had Rose contacted the killer to ask about it?

As Red spoke with the state police, Myrtle mulled over her next move. It was probably time to pay another call on Claudia Brown. She'd seemed very earnest when she'd told Myrtle she'd look out for Pasha. Who knew—maybe she'd even had a Pasha sighting? Besides, the way Maxine had talked, she thought perhaps Claudia was more upset over losing her soloist position at the church than Myrtle had realized.

"Mama?" Red's voice interrupted her thoughts. "The folks from the state police would like to ask you a few questions." Myrtle walked toward the group of officers and Red muttered to her, "Probably want to hear firsthand how you keep finding dead bodies everywhere."

Actually, the state police had not asked her such a rude question. Myrtle's favorite SBI policeman, Detective Lieutenant Perkins, had been on the scene and had listened carefully to every word she said, sometimes jotting down a note or two in a small notebook. He seemed to accept Myrtle's story without question. He was interested more in the time of her arrival, the noise she'd heard in the kitchen, and whether she'd seen the escaping murderer. Then he'd politely thanked her and let her go.

"Do you need a ride somewhere, Mama?" asked Red in a rushed manner.

"Won't you be tied up here for a while?" asked Myrtle.

"Not necessarily. The state police are pretty capable of ..." He broke off as Perkins called him to come over.

"Never mind," said Myrtle. "I think you're going to end up more tied up here than you think. A walk will be good for me and give me the chance to keep an eye out for Pasha, too." And to talk to Claudia Brown without Red being difficult.

Claudia didn't seem excited to see her. Actually, Claudia Brown seemed completely appalled to see Myrtle. Her always-tightly-permed mousy hair was practically standing up on end and she looked as though she had been doing yard work. Very diligent yard work according to the amount of perspiration that appeared to have been generated.

"Miss Myrtle," said Claudia weakly. "Hi. What are you doing here?"

"My dear, I've had a simply terrible morning. Terrible! I need some consolation."

Claudia stared blankly at her.

"Consolation," repeated Myrtle slowly. When that engendered no response, Myrtle rephrased. "I need someone to invite me in and offer me lemonade."

"Oh!" Claudia finally nodded her understanding. "Come on in, Miss Myrtle. Have a seat."

She led Myrtle into her small and very untidy living room where she hurriedly made room for her on a sofa covered with what looked like scrapbooking supplies and bits of fabric. "You're crafty," said Myrtle. "How very impressive." The room, if it were possible, was even more cluttered than it had appeared the last time Myrtle stood in it.

Claudia seemed as if she were trying to hold onto a thought. This was apparently a painful process, judging from her squished-up face. Finally, she said, "Lemonade. That's right. I'll get it."

"Or just water, if that's what you have," called Myrtle behind her as Claudia trotted off to the kitchen.

Myrtle took the opportunity to glance around her a bit. There was so much clutter that it was a bit overwhelming. It was easy to find a clue in a house like Rose Mayfield's, where everything had a special spot...and was *in* its special spot. In a house like Claudia's, however, it was a different story. Claudia did have pictures, unlike Rose. In fact, Claudia had so many pictures that it was difficult to absorb them all. There were pictures of what must be Claudia's parents, pictures of what looked to be a Sunday school class. Pictures everywhere and the frames appeared to have been personally matted by Claudia herself.

Myrtle reached across to the scrapbook next to her on the sofa. It was full of church bulletins. Upon further investigation, Myrtle noted that Claudia was mentioned in each and every one of the bulletins that she opened. *Soloist Claudia Brown.* She even had a couple of newspaper clippings that mentioned her singing at the church. Well, that just goes to show the kind of newspaper that Myrtle wrote for. *The Bradley Bugle* was nothing if not a small town paper.

She heard Claudia returning and quickly pulled back from the scrapbook, instead gazing innocently out the window as she approached with a glass of lemonade and a single ice cube.

She'd filled the glass all the way to the rim, which was particularly shortsighted since she'd known she'd have to walk with it. Sure enough, the resulting sloshing over the rim as Claudia approached meant for a sticky glass. Claudia hadn't brought a napkin with her...and seemed rather oddly oblivious to the spill.

"Here we are," said Claudia brightly. She sat down next to Myrtle, perching on the bit of sofa that appeared after she'd shoved the scrapbook farther away. She gazed uncertainly at Myrtle through her cat eye glasses and shifted a bit uncomfortably. "Are you having a good day?"

Myrtle gave Claudia her best, reassuring, old-lady smile. Claudia appeared even mousier than she usually did. Today she wore a brown top *and* brown slacks. She didn't want to scare off this woman before she'd even started really asking her questions, but she was here for a reason.

"It's been a difficult day, I'm sorry to say. Very difficult. You see, I discovered Rose Mayhew's dead body in her house this morning." Myrtle pursed her lips primly and sat up straight in her seat.

Claudia gave a ragged gasp and clutched her throat. But there was a flash, just for a fraction of a second, of some unidentifiable emotion in her ordinarily-dull eyes. "Did Rose have a...heart attack?" asked Claudia in a hopeful voice.

"She did not. She had a murderer attack her with a fireplace poker." Myrtle made her voice as grim and schoolteacher-like as possible. Some people responded well to this tactic and she hoped that Claudia would. There were actually many things Myrtle would like to tell Claudia in her schoolteacher voice. Sit up straight, don't bite your nails, and stop pulling your earlobes or else they'll reach down to your knees. Being around Claudia made Myrtle agitated.

Claudia was looking rather green. "Murdered?"

"I'm afraid so," said Myrtle briskly. She leveled a look at Claudia. "What were you doing this morning?"

"*This* morning?" asked Claudia frantically.

"This morning."

"Yard work. I was doing yard work." Claudia's nail bitten hand stopped pulling her ear lobe and clutched her throat again.

"Oh, excellent!" Myrtle gave Claudia a bright smile. "Wonderful, that's truly wonderful. So then you can tell me if you saw anything suspicious."

Claudia frowned in puzzlement.

"Maybe you saw someone acting suspiciously in the neighborhood? Someone disheveled as if they'd been bolting through wooded areas, maybe?"

Claudia hesitated. "I'm not really sure."

"Or, perhaps, you've seen Pasha? Since you've been outside such a long time, I mean."

Now Claudia looked truly concerned. "Pasha? Is someone missing?"

"Pasha is my cat," said Myrtle, slowly. "Remember? I came by here with some flyers. You said you'd look out for her."

"Oh, yes! Right. The white cat."

"The black cat," said Myrtle tersely.

Claudia just shook her head miserably.

"Look, have you seen or noticed *anything*?" Myrtle could feel frustration welling up in her like heartburn. "When did you last see Rose?"

"Not since book club," said Claudia quickly. Maybe too quickly.

Myrtle was getting nowhere. She chose a slightly different tack. "And, by the way, everyone thinks you were wildly jealous of Naomi Pelter. That you resented her upstaging you in the choir. Can you speak to that?"

Claudia burst into tears. Myrtle, never one to handle crying well, glanced around the cluttered room for a box of tissues. Seeing none, she dug in her gigantic pocketbook. All she could come up with was a tissue she'd used to blot her lipstick. "Here," she mumbled, "this is clean. I only used it for my makeup." She sighed. If only Miles had been here. He'd have given her one of those warning looks of his that were so handy when Myrtle was about to accidentally step over the line with a suspect interview.

Claudia took it gratefully and blew her nose resoundingly.

"So, tell me about it, dear. I understand that Naomi wasn't the nicest woman in the world. Was she mean to you?" Myrtle felt as if she were back in the classroom, trying to help a student deal with a bully.

Claudia's eyes were still full of tears. "That's what makes it so awful. Naomi was always so nice to me! So very sweet."

Myrtle sincerely doubted this. What she felt more sure of was that poor Claudia was too naïve to pick out false praise.

"Naomi always told me what a great singer I was and how privileged she felt to sing in the same choir as me. But Naomi–" It seemed to pain Claudia to continue. She swallowed hard. "She was a much better singer than I am."

"Oh. Well, I doubt that," said Myrtle brusquely.

"No, it's true. She had the voice of an angel. It was amazing," said Claudia slowly. She appeared dumbfounded just contemplating Naomi's skill.

"Are you back to being the lead soloist now?" asked Myrtle. "Has the choir director spoken with you at all about it?"

Claudia flushed and gave a quick shoulder shrug. "It was one of those things that sort of went without saying. Since I was the lead before Naomi was."

"And now you feel bad because you're the lead again."

"All of my problems were fixed when Naomi died," Claudia said softly. "I have only one talent. Only one gift. I'm not pretty or smart or good at things. Naomi was all of those things and more. Once she decided she wanted to sing in the choir...my whole life was turned upside-down. My singing was the only thing that people were kind to me about. Now things are better again...and I feel so guilty."

Myrtle studied her. Yes, she did feel guilty. But she also felt joy—a gladness. You could see it in her. And, really, who could blame her? "Can you think of anyone who might have wanted to get rid of Naomi?"

"Isn't that what we should be asking about Rose? Shouldn't we be wondering who might have wanted to get rid of her?" asked Claudia, twisting her tissue in her hand.

"I have a feeling that Rose was murdered because she knew who killed Naomi. So once we find out who murdered Naomi, we'll know who murdered Rose."

Claudia frowned as if she'd forgotten what the original question was.

"Can you think of someone who might have wanted Naomi dead?" asked Myrtle with more patience than she was feeling.

"Oh. Well, Maxine," said Claudia. She made a bit of a face when she said the name, as if it was sour in her mouth.

"Maxine didn't like Naomi?"

"No. Not at all." Claudia paused, but when Myrtle was clearly waiting for more explanation, she reluctantly continued. "Some sort of a love thing. I really don't know." And Claudia gave a wave of her hand to indicate that she wasn't at all sure how complex love triangles operated.

Myrtle pushed up with one hand on the seat of the sofa and stood up. She saw a flash of relief on Claudia's face as Myrtle got ready to leave.

"I'll be sure to look out for your dog," said Claudia in a hurry, standing up herself.

Myrtle gave a tight smile. "It's a cat. Pasha. A black cat."

"Yes, that's right. A black cat."

Myrtle said in a casual voice, "I suppose I'll see you soon—maybe at garden club. I've been terrible at attending lately. Dreadful. But you've been to the last couple of meetings, haven't you?"

Claudia said, "I go to all the meetings. The ones for book club, too. I don't get out much, otherwise."

It had a ring of truth to it. Myrtle added, "You're good to go. I'm always just worried that I'm going to get stuck next to someone I don't want to talk to. Like Erma Sherman."

Myrtle shuddered and this made a smile tug at the corners of Claudia's mouth.

Myrtle continued, "Haven't they been trying to do some sort of seating arrangements, too? Elaine was telling me about it one time. Place cards. That means I'd really be trapped."

"Just at their luncheons and things. But if you don't like where you're sitting, you can pick up your place card and trade with someone else. When no one's looking," said Claudia earnestly.

"Really? And you've seen people do this?" asked Myrtle.

Claudia flushed again. "It's okay. People do it."

"Did you see anyone do it at the garden club luncheon?" asked Myrtle intently.

Claudia flushed even redder and violently shook her head, making her small curls jiggle on top of her head.

Had Rose Mayfield seen something like this happen? Except the motivation wasn't to escape a horrendous bore like Erma Sherman—but to slip a poisonous mushroom into a salad?

Chapter Eleven

After leaving Claudia's house, Myrtle walked rather slowly in the direction of home, trying to organize her thoughts as she walked. Unfortunately, at one point she wasn't really watching where she was treading and stepped into some gravel on the sidewalk, that made her stumble. She was glaring at the gravel and kicking it to the side with her foot when she heard a car drive up behind her.

Myrtle turned quickly, thinking it must be Miles again, spying and seeing her walking with difficulty. But it was Maxine Tristan. She rolled her window down and called out, "You all right? Hop in. I'll drive you wherever you want to go."

Myrtle was irritated at being caught stumbling and almost refused the help...but then realized that this was a good way to do a quick follow-up with Maxine. She'd talked to Maxine only yesterday—but yesterday Rose Mayfield had been alive. And now there was the fact that Claudia had pointed a finger at Maxine. Plenty to talk over. She forced a smile on her face and said, "That's very kind of you, Maxine. I'll take you up on that. I'm heading back home."

Myrtle plopped down in Maxine's front seat. This was a difficult task because this was what would be considered a *cute* car. Cute cars had no backseats to speak of, not much of a front seat, were low to the ground, were oddly shaped, and were stick shift. Myrtle wondered if she might require a forklift to get back out of the front seat.

Plus, Maxine seemed to be smoking again. And in the small confines of this *cute* vehicle, Myrtle wouldn't be able to escape the fumes. She glared ferociously at the offending article and Maxine hastily stubbed it out. "Don't like cigarettes? Really? I thought everyone your age smoked or used to smoke, Miss Myrtle."

"I'm not everyone," said Myrtle.

"You're not. That's why I like you," said Maxine.

Myrtle hurried on, since the drive home would be a short one. "Thanks for the ride, Maxine. I guess I'm more decrepit than I ordinarily would be...since it's been such a trying day."

She peered sideways at Maxine, but Maxine was fiddling with her cell phone, which alarmed Myrtle even more than the cigarette had. Really, she needed to remove herself from this death trap of a vehicle as soon as possible. She coughed to try to capture Maxine's attention again.

Maxine finally put the phone down into a cup holder and glanced Myrtle's way. "What was that again? Sorry. Did you say you had a bad day? What's happened?"

What *hadn't* happened? But Myrtle, considering the shortness of the drive said, "I discovered Rose Mayfield's dead body this morning."

"*What?*" Maxine turned to look fully at Myrtle and turned the wheel of the cute car at the same time until they scraped the curb and Maxine corrected it. "Rose is dead? What happened?"

"Someone killed her in her own living room with her fireplace poker," said Myrtle in her best what-a-shame voice.

"What is going on here?" asked Maxine under her breath. "Surely Bradley isn't the setting for a serial killer of some kind. So, did Rose somehow know something about Naomi's death?"

"That's what I think," said Myrtle simply, glad that Maxine had connected the dots and that she didn't have to do it for her.

"Well, I suppose your son and those guys from the state police will be asking questions," said Maxine. "I think they've finally come to the conclusion that I need to be considered as a possible suspect, because they checked in with me late yesterday about Naomi. When was it that Rose died? Hopefully, I have an alibi. Although I sincerely doubt it, since I live alone."

"Same with me," said Myrtle. "And it looks as if she died sometime early this morning."

"Same with you?" Maxine turned to grin at Myrtle as they pulled up in her driveway. "Surely you aren't a suspect? Age has got to have *some* benefits, hasn't it?"

"No, I guess I'm probably not a suspect." Irritating, thought Myrtle. "But I did discover both bodies and I knew both women. For heaven's sake, I *should* be a suspect."

Maxine seemed to be mulling things over as she put the car in park and leaned back in the driver's seat. "Let's see. Early this morning. Nope! I got nothin'. I was drinking coffee and reading my newspaper."

"No one saw you go get your paper or anything?" asked Myrtle.

"Doubt it. The paper carrier slings my paper nearly to the front door. I barely stick my nose out to retrieve it."

Myrtle frowned. "Well that's rather irritating. I'm sure we have the same carrier. And I have to walk nearly to the street. I am frequently forced to talk to Erma Sherman right when the sun is coming up, and that's a real pity let me assure you. I may have to leave a note for my newspaper carrier at the *Bradley Bugle* office the next time I'm there."

Maxine grinned at Myrtle smugly. It made Myrtle think that Maxine had spent some time flirting with the newspaper carrier simply to produce that effect. Very annoying of the carrier. *Age before beauty*. That was the saying. Didn't he know that?

"Maxine, could you tell me a little more about this issue you had with Naomi? It was over a love affair, wasn't it?" asked Myrtle. Her voice was a bit brusque, which she hadn't intended. It was all because of the news carrier.

Maxine lifted a well-shaped eyebrow. "Are you one of those gossipy old ladies, Miss Myrtle? I wouldn't have thought that of you."

"Let's just say that I have a fondness for a good old-fashioned soap opera. Like *Tomorrow's Promise*. Maybe that's why I'm interested," said Myrtle smoothly.

"Ah. *Tomorrow's Promise*. Torrid romance and plenty of melodrama. How did you even know Naomi and I had fallen out over a love affair?" asked Maxine. "Did someone say something to you about it?" She paused. "Claudia perhaps?"

Myrtle ignored the question. "So what happened, then? Did Naomi steal away some man you cared about?"

Maxine looked longingly at the pack of cigarettes on the center console. "Yes, she did. She didn't merely steal away *one* man I cared about. It was a pattern of behavior for her. She would steal away *every* man I dated. She saw it as a sort of game I think. But the last time she did it she really stepped over the line. I was engaged you see, Miss Myrtle."

Myrtle nodded. She'd thought it might be something like that.

"He was a fine man—handsome, funny. He had a truly wonderful job. I'd never have had to work a day more in my life. And Naomi didn't care two figs for him. You could see those two were clearly unsuited. Naomi was fun-loving, impulsive. John was serious, thoughtful."

"Thoughtful. And yet he threw over his fiancée for a fling?" Myrtle frowned. There was something that didn't seem right.

"It was a game for Naomi. She was bored. She had this amazing ability to morph into anything for anyone...she could get along with anyone if she'd wanted to. She could have even charmed Rose Mayfield into thinking she was wonderful. But Naomi would only turn on the charm when she had a real motive. Making me furious was a real motive. She saw me as her only real competition in town and made it a point of honor to ruin any relationship I had." Maxine reached over for another cigarette. Then she paused in mid-air and reluctantly reeled in her hand.

"What ended up happening?" asked Myrtle. "To John, I mean. It didn't seem to me that Naomi had a boyfriend when she died. And you're—well ...."

"I'm alone," finished Maxine dryly. "Yes. What happened to John is that he fell deeply in love with Naomi...or Naomi's persona that she adopted. As soon as he'd ended our engagement, Naomi dropped him like a hot potato. After all, they had nothing in common."

"And John?"

"He left town. Took off to practice law in Charlotte. Gone. Heartbroken. I know how he felt," she said, the flippant voice gone, replaced with a bitter one.

"And now she's dead. So no more competitions for lovers' attention," said Myrtle.

"She's dead. Praise be," said Maxine levelly. "But I had nothing to do with it. I'd have put my money on Rose. Now that Rose is dead, I'd have to pick Claudia for the killer."

"Claudia?" Myrtle still was having a hard time reconciling clumsy Claudia for a cold-blooded murderer.

"Sure. Why not? Haven't you heard that still waters run deep? Oh, you'd *think* it would be me, right? I've got plenty of motive. I'm brassy enough to kill people with fireplace pokers and poisons. I'm more of the obvious choice, don't you think?"

Myrtle quickly agreed with her since Maxine was making restless movements that meant Myrtle's time in her car was running out. "You're right. It's probably someone who has a motive we haven't even uncovered yet."

"Judging from Naomi, the motives are likely legion," drawled Maxine.

"Thanks for the ride," said Myrtle, beaming her helpless old-lady smile at Maxine. "It's been fun talking. I do hope we can talk again soon. Maybe at garden club? I really need to make a meeting since I've missed so very many. Have you gone to garden club the last couple of times?"

"I sure have," said Maxine. "If only to stare daggers at Naomi."

Myrtle was about to ask her about seating arrangements when Maxine said, "Do you need any help getting out, Miss Myrtle? I've got such a tiny car that it might be hard to extract yourself—and I know you're ready to go in."

Myrtle blinked at her in confusion.

"It's two o'clock," Maxine said smoothly. "Time for *Tomorrow's Promise.*"

Myrtle did watch *Tomorrow's Promise*. Mainly, she watched it to clear her brain. She had so many ideas and bits of clues and gossip floating around in her head that she felt she needed a break from it. Somehow, though, after listening to Maxine talk about her love triangle with Naomi, the soap opera seemed rather tame in comparison.

After the soap was over, she sat in her chair, thinking. Myrtle still wanted to talk with Lena, the vet, again—both about Rose's death and also to ask her about Pasha again. She needed to check in with her about Rose's death and where she was this morning. She also wanted to find out if she'd been to those two vitally important garden club meetings where Destroying Angel was first introduced to the group and then would most-likely have been dispensed to Naomi Pelter. And whether she'd spotted anyone deliberately changing seats to be next to Naomi.

But Myrtle also knew she had her limits. Lena's office was a decent ways away—she'd need a ride. Miles was angry with her, which was unfortunate.

She suddenly realized that she'd left the sprinkler on since she'd left that morning to talk to Rose. Myrtle muttered something dire under her breath and hurried out to cut it off. Mud was everywhere and she'd wasted water. Shoot.

Myrtle carefully scraped the mud off her shoes on the mat and walked back inside just as the phone started ringing. "Hello?" asked Myrtle, as she picked it up.

"Myrtle? It's Elaine." Myrtle could hear an exhausted-sounding toddler wailing in the background.

"Elaine? How are you?"

Elaine gave a short laugh. "Myrtle, that's what I've called to ask *you*! Red told me that you discovered Rose Mayfield's body this morning. I was so sorry to hear it."

"Because you liked Rose so much?" asked Myrtle, crinkling her brow. She couldn't recall Elaine and Rose being particularly close. In fact, she wasn't sure she'd ever heard Elaine even mention Rose's name before.

"No, because I like *you* so much! You have this habit of tripping over dead people. It must have scared you to death this morning," said Elaine. She then heard Elaine saying to Jack, "Mama is on the phone, Jack! Here's your sippy cup. Is that what you wanted?" Myrtle heard the sound of what she interpreted as the sippy cup hitting Elaine's kitchen floor.

"It was a little scary, yes. Especially since Rose's body was in the same spot that Naomi's had been."

"And Red said the murderer was still in Rose's house! Terrifying." The volume of the crying on Elaine's end grew exponentially.

Elaine wouldn't want to help her investigate—not with Red on the warpath the way he'd been about Myrtle snooping around in his cases. But she wouldn't mind helping her find Pasha—after all, she'd been very helpful with the picture for the poster. She could tell Elaine that she needed to follow-up with Lena on the flyers she put out there.

"Elaine, do you have any errands to run this afternoon? Because I don't want to make you go out if you don't have to."

"Right this second, I would *love* to get out, Myrtle. Jack has acted possessed all day. I don't know what is going on with the poor guy." Elaine's voice was frazzled and sounded a bit sleep-deprived.

A possessed toddler. This didn't sound good. And somehow Lena Fowler didn't exactly seem like the kind of woman who took well to screaming toddlers. Myrtle frowned. Elaine seemed to be waiting for a response of some kind from her. What was it she'd been saying? Oh, right—wondering what's going on with Jack? Myrtle tried to remember the pertinent details of screaming toddlers, but had to reach back in her memory about forty-five years. "Teeth?" she said vaguely.

"Maybe it's teeth. Or maybe his stomach hurts. I'm just not sure."

The sounds of unadulterated toddler fury continued. Myrtle adored her grandson. He was a wonderful, wonderful little boy. She loved it when they played with his toy trucks and when she read his favorite book with him. She just wasn't altogether sure that she wanted to spend time with him under the present circumstances.

"I know what we can do. I can drop you off at your errand and wait in the car. Then we can drive over to the new cross-stitch shop downtown," said Elaine in a loud voice that could be heard over the screaming.

Myrtle winced. "Cross-stitch?" Surely Elaine wasn't trying to foist her latest hobby on Myrtle again? She hadn't the interest nor the eyesight to make the tiny little *x*s required for cross-stitch.

"I mean—*I* would go into the cross-stitch store and you would stay out in the car. With Jack. You know...so I wouldn't have to take him in there."

Judging from the shrieking Myrtle heard in the background, she could only pray that by that time Jack would have fallen asleep in his car seat from sheer exhaustion. "Of course, Elaine. I'd be happy to."

"What?" asked Elaine over the racket.

"I'd be happy to! Delighted! Yes!" Myrtle's voice rivaled Jack's in volume.

"See you in ten minutes!" yelled Elaine.

So it was with great trepidation that Myrtle locked her front door behind her, squared her shoulders, and strode toward Elaine's minivan. But to her relief, Jack beamed at her as soon as she cautiously opened the passenger door.

"What a love! You love to see your Nana, don't you?" Myrtle cooed at Jack. Then she carefully settled into the front seat. "What did you do?" she asked Elaine in a low voice. "Perform an exorcism?"

"Just about. I finally figured out that the word he was repeating was crackers. I couldn't figure out what he was saying through all the howling. Once I gave him some graham crackers, we were A-OK." Elaine looked over her shoulder as she backed out of Myrtle's driveway.

"I wish my problems were as easily solved," said Myrtle gloomily.

Elaine gave her a sympathetic wince. "Red told me you were on the outs with Miles. What happened?"

Myrtle sighed. "Nothing, really. It was all silly. I was in a frustrated mood and I threw an accusation at him."

Elaine's eyes widened. "An accusation? Against Miles? What on earth did he do?"

"Well. I told him he didn't care anything about Pasha."

Elaine thought on this for a moment. "He probably doesn't, does he? I think I remember hearing about a couple of occasions when he was viciously attacked by Pasha."

"Pasha was very protective of me," said Myrtle stoutly.

"So Miles doesn't care anything about Pasha," said Elaine slowly, "but he does care about you. And he cared about your worries and your problems. So, from that viewpoint, he *did* care about Pasha."

Myrtle pressed her lips together. If there was one thing she disliked, it was being in the wrong. She had snapped at Miles, it was true. Now she supposed she'd have to go to him, hat in hand, and apologize. At some point. It was all very irritating.

Elaine decided to let the topic be, which was just as well since they were pulling into the veterinarian's office. "All right, so I'll stay in the car with Jack and you can run in and ask Dr. Fowler about Pasha."

It was also annoying not to really have a sidekick for these interviews. Perhaps she'd have to make up with Miles earlier than she thought. "What do you think of Lena Fowler, by the way? What's your impression of her?"

Elaine looked confused. "As a vet, you mean? But we don't have pets at our house."

"No, I mean as a person. She's in garden club and book club with us, you know—what do you think about her?" Myrtle shifted her cane to help her get out of the van.

"Oh, goodness, I haven't been to club meetings regularly for so long—you know I can go only on Jack's preschool days. I mean, I *do* know Lena. But she's not really in my peer group. I suppose I think that she's tough, doesn't suffer fools lightly, smart, no-nonsense. Athletic. And she probably gets along better with animals than she does with people." Elaine absently handed Jack a sandwich bag full of toasted oats cereal.

Elaine was more perceptive than she thought. It's a shame Red had been so adamant about Myrtle not being involved in this particular case. Elaine would never consent to acting as a backup sidekick, and it was a pity...she would be a good one.

Chapter Twelve

It was surprisingly quiet in the vet's office. Usually it was bustling with people. The receptionist didn't appear to be out front, either. Myrtle frowned.

A bell had sounded on the door when Myrtle walked in, so she figured someone knew she was there. She waited in the reception area for a minute or two. Finally, Lena strode into the reception area. "Oh. Mrs. Clover. Sorry to keep you waiting."

"No staff today?" asked Myrtle, looking around.

"Cindy had to take the afternoon off for a doctor appointment," said Lena brusquely. "What can I help you with?"

She certainly was one to always get to the point in a hurry. It was usually a trait that Myrtle admired, too. Just not so much when she was trying to get to the bottom of a mystery. Fortunately, Myrtle had the ability to get right to the point, too.

"Was Cindy also gone early this morning? I know your office opens early."

"We open at six for scheduled surgeries to get those completed before we open the doors for regular appointments," said Lena smoothly.

"And did you have surgeries this morning?" asked Myrtle.

"As a matter of fact, we didn't. Too bad, since we had several yesterday and will have a couple tomorrow. Some days it simply works out that way. I wish they could be more spread out." Lena examined Myrtle through narrowed eyes. "Why are you so curious about my surgery schedule? Have you found Pasha?"

"Not yet. Was Cindy helping this morning, then?"

Lena began to look impatient. "She wasn't, no. Why would she, with no scheduled surgeries? She came in late as a matter of fact. Why do you want to know?"

"Because Rose Mayfield was murdered early this morning in her home. I was curious where various people were during that time."

Lena took a small step back from Myrtle as if trying to distance herself physically from the implied accusation. "Well. I'm sorry to hear about Rose. But her death has nothing to do with me. I respected Rose and have known her for years. What possible reason could I have to want her dead?"

Myrtle said in a musing tone, "I suppose the only reason you'd want her dead is if she threatened to expose you for murdering Naomi Pelter. Then Rose would represent a risk to be eliminated."

Lena stared at her with her large, intelligent brown eyes set in her serious face. "Yes. If I'd murdered Naomi, and Rose indicated she was going to alert everyone, then I suppose I would want her out of the way. Of course, considering I had nothing to do with Naomi's death, it means that I'd never have murdered Rose." She gave Myrtle a piercing look. "Does Chief Clover realize that you're out here nosing around?"

And, with a cold certainty, Myrtle realized the danger that Lena Fowler presented. She was a lot like Myrtle, actually. She had a low tolerance for nonsense. And she'd believe that what Myrtle was doing was nonsense—and, possibly, something potentially harmful to herself. Lena would think nothing of picking up a phone and tersely informing Red that Myrtle was checking into these murders...just to shut Myrtle down.

Myrtle's realization must have played out on Lena's face because she said, more gently this time, "Good luck finding Pasha. I know you're worried about her, but I promise you that she's probably just fine. Cats can get disoriented if they're even slightly off their home turf so that's a possibility. She may not be sure how to get back home to you, even if she's geographically very close. Or else she might be lying low until the coast is clear. In either case, she's likely just fine. I'm sure I'll see you soon. At garden club, maybe?"

Myrtle quickly asked, "Have you gone to the last couple of meetings? I mean, I feel as if I don't know what's going on with that club since I haven't attended for a while."

Lena gave her a sharp look. "Yes, I've happened to make the last couple of meetings—sometimes my schedule unexpectedly opens up."

"I've heard they're pushing seating arrangements there. That's one of the reasons I haven't made it since I don't want to be forced to sit next to Erma Sherman for an hour or more. Although maybe I could switch place cards with someone. Have you ever noticed anyone doing that?" Myrtle widened her eyes innocently at Lena.

The door chimed behind them and a short, chubby woman walked in carrying a small, excited dog. "I'll see you soon, Miss Myrtle," said Lena dismissively, moving to greet the woman.

Unfortunately, Possessed Jack had returned in the interim and Myrtle winced as she got into Elaine's van. The volume of crying was loud enough that Elaine had opened the windows to let the sound go somewhere other than in their ears. They drove in tense silence (well, except for Jack) to the cross-stitch store. "I'll be right back," said Elaine loudly, with an apologetic look at Myrtle. She hurried into the store.

Myrtle opened the passenger door and then tugged at the van's rear door until it slid open. A tearful Jack blinked at her in surprise. Never one to let even a momentary advantage pass unused, Myrtle said, "Hi there, Jack! Nana is so glad to see you! Here, I brought something for you to play with for a few minutes while Mama shops."

Now she rooted around desperately in her pocketbook for something for Jack to play with. Her hands closed around a small cylindrical object and she pulled it out to find it was Wanda's pepper spray. She hastily shoved it back into her purse. "One minute, just a minute," she mumbled, hoping her placating tone would hold Jack off from any future wailing.

Then she pulled out her cell phone. Would Jack even want to play with her phone? She looked doubtfully at it. Elaine had a fancy phone and Jack wasn't allowed to touch it in case he accidentally reprogrammed it or something. Myrtle's phone was a basic flip phone that looked like something the dinosaurs might have placed their calls on. She shrugged and handed it over to the toddler. Jack was expecting *something* and Myrtle's pocket-book didn't seem to have much magic in it today.

Luckily, Jack seemed mesmerized by the strangeness of the archaic device. He turned it over and over in his hands. Then he discovered that it flipped up to reveal the numbers and he gazed at the device with rapt attention. And the fact that he was hitting buttons like crazy didn't even worry Myrtle since Red had set up a lock on the phone when he'd gotten it for her. Cops are security conscious like that.

Elaine strode rapidly back toward the car, a worried crease on her forehead and a bag in her hand. Her frown eased when she couldn't hear screaming emanating from the vehicle. "Miracle worker," she breathed to Myrtle as she got into the car. Then she looked concerned again. "He's not dialing China is he?"

"It's got a lock code on there, so he can dial numbers all day," said Myrtle. For the first time, she was glad to have the annoying passcode.

"Now we can actually hear ourselves talk," said Elaine in relief. "Did Lena Fowler have any information about Pasha?"

Myrtle shifted in her seat a bit guiltily. Then she remembered that she and the vet actually had discussed Pasha. In a rather incidental way, but still. "Lena said that Pasha might be lying low until she thinks the coast is clear. That, or else she may be disoriented by being even slightly away from her usual stomping ground. She might not be far away, but ran just far enough to get away from the dogs that she isn't exactly sure where she is or how to get back."

"Aren't there all those stories about cats making incredible journeys back home?" asked Elaine.

"I guess it depends on the cat. Or something. I don't know...maybe dogs are really the ones who have the internal GPS. Aren't those usually stories about dogs? Anyway, Lena made me feel a little better." *That and the fact that Wanda had said that Pasha was okay.* But Myrtle would keep that information to herself. She certainly didn't need to let Elaine know that she'd gone out to see Wanda. That was always an indicator that Myrtle was working on a case.

Myrtle peered at Elaine. "How are you doing? This is a real rough patch for being a parent. Late nights, early mornings, uncertain naptimes. Are you holding on to your sanity?" She summoned her courage and said in a firm voice, "Because if you need a break, of any kind, you know you can always bring Jack by to play with me. Miles was telling me just the other day that I've got just as much energy as a toddler. So we know I can keep up with Jack, you see."

Elaine appeared to be choking up a little, much to Myrtle's discomfort. She quickly regained control, however, and flashed a smile at Myrtle. "You don't know how much I appreciate that, Myrtle. Believe me—if I need you, I have no compunction about giving you a call. You know that Jack loves spending time with his Nana. It's going pretty well...it's challenging being a mother, but I love it."

"And you're keeping up with outside interests, too. With the cross-stitch. That's so important."

Elaine said, "I'm trying. Some days I don't really make any progress with my pattern. There are also the days when I have to pick my pattern up and put it down a million times to keep Jack from pulling down a lamp by the cord or climbing up a bookcase." She gave a rueful smile.

Myrtle could only imagine what a pattern that had been picked up and put down a lot might look like…if you were a distracted mother. And poor Elaine didn't have the best track record for arts and crafts.

Elaine gave her a sideways glance. "You mentioned Miles a minute ago. I hope y'all do make up soon. I know what good friends you are. Pasha's a wonderful cat, but not everyone might understand that. Or even understand cats, period."

Myrtle nodded. "It all just boiled down to squabbling between friends. Sometimes it happens." She felt a pang, though, which she quickly suppressed.

"Well, you and Miles do spend a lot of time together. You're bound to get on each other's nerves." Elaine pulled up into Myrtle's driveway.

"Thanks for driving me out there," said Myrtle.

"Thanks for calming Jack down," said Elaine with a sigh. "I think I'm going to try to put him down for a nap as soon as we get home. He's got to be worn out with all the crying."

As if on cue, Jack wailed again.

Myrtle discovered that Jack wasn't the only one who was exhausted from the events of the day. When she started feeling sleepy, she looked at her living room clock to find that it was only eight o'clock. But Myrtle was the last one to turn down an opportunity to sleep on the rare times sleepiness presented itself to her. She stuck another can of tuna outside, even if it ended up being raccoons that she fed, and put on her nightgown. She was fast asleep within five minutes.

It was two o'clock in the morning when she awakened. Myrtle was never surprised at waking up at two. It was a standard time when she ordinarily glanced at her bedside table clock. This time, though, her awakening was accompanied by an odd, unsettled feeling. She lay still in her bed, listening intently. Could it be Pasha outside? She'd heard a noise, hadn't she?

Then Myrtle heard it again. It wasn't a very catlike sound, though. Pasha wouldn't be jiggling her back door handle. Was that what she was hearing? Myrtle swung her legs out of bed and slowly stood up, putting her arms through the robe she had placed on the foot of her bed and shoving her feet in a pair of slippers. Her pocketbook was in the armchair near her bed and she rummaged in it for Wanda's pepper spray. Grabbing it, she pushed her bedroom door wider and peered out.

And saw a hooded figure tugging at her back door as if to open it.

Chapter Thirteen

The figure froze. Myrtle froze. And then the figure took off running.

Myrtle hurried to the kitchen door, yelling, "Stop!" and gripping her pepper spray as if she'd never let go. She flung open the back door and hurried outside in time to see the dark figure running out her gate in the direction of the woods around the lake. She bellowed again, "Stop!" There was no way she could catch up with anyone moving that fast...and who was almost certainly decades younger than she was. But then the figure stumbled over a tree root and went down...and Myrtle started hurrying toward the intruder again.

A bit of movement near her legs made her jump and she looked down in time only to see an emaciated, dirty Pasha gazing up at her in terror with her fur raised. The running, the screaming...clearly the cat was scared to death. "Pasha," she gasped in joy. She thought no more about the figure bolting through the woods as she stooped down to reach out soothingly to the animal. "Here kitty," she called.

But Pasha was well and truly spooked and bolted away into the darkness, tearing off through the gate.

Myrtle stood still, hoping that Pasha would come back in a few minutes. But she didn't.

The next morning, after restless wakefulness for the rest of the night, Myrtle discovered that not only had the intruder escaped, not only had Pasha gotten away, but she'd tracked mud all over her house because her yard had been so soggy from leaving the sprinkler running. It was time for her luck to change, it really was. The only bright spot was that she had *seen* Pasha with her own eyes. The poor thing was alive, if not in the best condition. And that made her feel better.

There was no way around it. She was going to have to call in the troops to clean this mess up. Well, actually, it was one troop. Puddin. Puddin was a sorry housekeeper, but Myrtle couldn't get rid of her because her husband, Dusty, was the only yardman in town who'd cut her grass even if her gnome collection was in the yard. So Myrtle put up with all kinds of nonsense from Puddin just to stay in Dusty's good graces. Although, Dusty wasn't exactly a prize, either.

Myrtle picked up the phone and called their house. As usual, Dusty picked up the phone. "Too dry ter mow, Miz Myrtle!" he hollered as soon as he heard her voice.

Myrtle gritted her teeth. Dusty was the laziest yardman alive. You'd think he didn't need the money the way he carried on. "I'm actually looking for Puddin, Dusty, so don't worry. The grass has stopped growing because of the heat, sure enough." Although, the backyard was sure to start growing again soon with all the watering she'd done.

"Puddin!" yelled Dusty. And then he dropped the phone with a clunk onto whatever surface was near him.

Minutes passed. Finally, a sour voice muttered, "H'lo?"

"Puddin? It's Myrtle Clover. I need your help today with some cleaning."

"Ain't on the schedule," said Puddin aggressively.

Myrtle was starting to be concerned that her teeth would sustain permanent damage from all the gritting she was doing. And she was very proud of her teeth. "Today isn't on the schedule, no, but you were supposed to come last week and didn't—so today can be a make-up day."

"Because my back was thrown out!"

"Yes, I remember the medical basis of your excuse. But I'm sure you're fine now—that was nearly a week ago," said Myrtle with as much patience as she could muster.

"Wellll." Puddin mulled this over. Myrtle could just picture her sullen, pasty face. "I suppose. What kinda cleaning are you looking for?"

Myrtle glanced over at the mud-streaked floor. "Oh, just some light cleaning. You know."

"None of that silver polishing!"

"No, not that," said Myrtle.

"All right," said Puddin. "I guess I could come now," she said in an ungrateful tone.

An hour later, Puddin stared in shock at the state of Myrtle's kitchen floor...and bedroom rug as a matter of fact. "Hey! What happened here?"

"There was a rare Pasha sighting," said Myrtle. "And a muddy backyard."

"That witch-cat ain't here, is she?" asked Puddin, swinging her head and peering around. Puddin, like Miles, was no fan of Pasha.

"No. But I think she might be coming home soon," said Myrtle.

Puddin gave her a dour look and pushed her lank, blonde hair out of her face. Then she filled up the sink and jerked the bottle of cleaner over it and stuck the mop inside. Without wringing out the mop, she swabbed at the floor resentfully.

Myrtle left Puddin alone to mop. There was another reason why she'd asked Puddin over—the housekeeper gossip network. In Bradley, there was this underworld of housekeeper intelligence. They bragged to each other about how much they knew about the lives of the people they cleaned for. Some of the time it was even true.

Mopping was pretty hard labor, too. Puddin would probably only be able to stand fifteen minutes of it before she was ready to talk. Myrtle simply sat in her living room and worked on the morning's crossword puzzle. And wondered over the fact that the Ural mountain range was in every single puzzle she'd done for the last week. Couldn't the puzzle designers have come up with other four-letter words?

Sure enough, it wasn't long before Puddin, sounding a bit breathless, joined her in the living room. "Hard work, Miz Myrtle," said Dutiful Puddin, pulling out a tissue from her jeans pocket and dramatically swabbing her pasty face. Myrtle noticed that Puddin's pale features weren't flushed from activity one smidgeon.

"Well, take a break for a moment, Puddin. Did you get it all done at least?"

"The mopping, anyway. What else you got for me?" Puddin's small eyes were watchful.

"Light cleaning, compared to the mud clean-up. A little dusting, collecting trash from the wastebaskets. And I wouldn't stop you if you put my laundry away."

Puddin relaxed a little. "No running the vacuum? No scrubbing the tub?"

"None of that today."

Puddin looked positively jolly now.

"While you're taking this short break," Myrtle put careful emphasis on *short*, "I wanted to ask you a couple of questions."

Puddin furrowed her brow. "Looking for the latest word on the street, is that right? Like the fact that Johnny Turrow done left his wife?"

Myrtle couldn't possibly care less about Johnny Turrow or his wife. "No, more if you have any information about Lena Fowler, Claudia Brown, or Maxine Tristan? Or maybe even Rose Mayfield?"

Puddin reported excitedly, in the tone of someone relaying news of great importance, "Rose Mayfield is dead!"

"Yes, that part I knew. I guess I was looking to see if there was anything about her that might have contributed to her death," said Myrtle.

Puddin appeared to be tripping over the word *contributed*. She finally gave up and said, "All I know is, she asked me to clean for her. I didn't even get there and she turned up dead. Sheila used to clean for her, but she got old and quit."

"Retired. Right. I remember Rose telling me that. She was looking for another housekeeper and Lord help me, I gave her your name. Did Sheila have anything to say about Rose Mayfield?" asked Myrtle.

"Sure thing. She got mad about the way Miz Mayfield told her she cut corners and stuff. Said if Miz Mayfield didn't like her cleaning, she could get out the bottle of glass cleaner and clean her own mirrors!"

Not very helpful. "I mean, did she say anything personally about Rose."

"She thought she was mean. And she complained a lot about her neighbors and acted like she was so perfect. But she wasn't. Sheila said that Miz Mayfield was trying to blackmail somebody." Puddin looked smug, knowing from Myrtle's face that she'd finally coughed up something good.

"That *Rose Mayfield* was trying to blackmail someone." Myrtle sat completely still to let the import of that statement seep through her. She could see Rose scolding someone about killing Naomi. She could even see Rose thanking the killer for murdering Naomi. What she couldn't see was Rose trying to sneak extra income from a killer. "How did Sheila come up with that? She wasn't working for Rose at the time of Naomi's death."

Puddin's already dumpy features sagged more. "She guessed it. But Sheila is a good guesser, Miz Myrtle. She said that Miz Mayfield's house was falling apart. It needed all kinds of repairs and Miz Mayfield only had enough money to pay her usual bills—nothing extra. The only reason she could pay for a cleaning lady is because she was too high and mighty to clean her own house. She even had a hard time coughing up the money for light bulbs. And Miz Mayfield loved that house. It was her mama's house, you know."

"Yes, I know about that," said Myrtle impatiently. "I was around, remember? I'm older than the hills. Okay, so no proof that Rose was blackmailing anyone, but an interesting theory floated by Sheila. What have you got for me on Claudia Brown?"

Puddin snickered. "What? Claudia Brown? Ain't nobody cleaning for her, Miz Myrtle. She's got no money for cleaning. And her house is a mess the likes of which nobody has ever seen."

Myrtle remembered the clutter on every surface and the scrapbook stuff on the sofa. "Nothing on Claudia, then. How about Lena Fowler and Maxine Tristan?"

"I clean Lena Fowler's office sometimes. Not that animal poop and stuff, but the other. Nobody cleans her house for her. I wanted to, so I didn't have to go near all them animals all the time but could clean a regular house. But she cleans her own house." Puddin made a face as if there was something fundamentally wrong about people who cleaned their own homes.

"What do you think about Doctor Fowler?" asked Myrtle.

"Oh, she's not a doctor. She just fixes up animals."

Myrtle gritted her teeth again. "Never mind. Tell me what you think of her. Had you heard anything about her husband and Naomi Pelter...anything like that?"

"I don't like her. Mean. Tells me I'm lazy." Puddin frowned in thought. "No! Says *slothful*. Tells me I'm *slothful*."

A straight shooter, that Lena.

"And I did hear about her husband and Naomi Pelter—that it was all nonsense. All Miz Fowler did was flirt with him to get him to fix stuff around her house for her. There weren't nothing interesting going on," Puddin said in a disgusted tone. "She's just mad cause her husband died, that's all. Ninny."

Myrtle couldn't think of anyone less like a ninny than stern Lena Fowler.

Puddin screwed up her face in thought. It was a painful process to watch. The Scholarly Puddin was impossible for her to pull off. "Lessee. Miz Maxine Tristan. She did have cleaning done sometimes, and then sometimes didn't have money and done cleaned herself." Puddin peered hopefully at Myrtle as if maybe she'd fulfilled her full gossip potential by merely sharing that Maxine's finances were sometimes unreliable.

Myrtle gave her a coolly unimpressed look.

Puddin sighed. "Miz Tristan. Lessee. I didn't clean for her, you know. She was another one of Sheila's ladies."

"Remember Sheila's thoughts on her at all?"

Puddin snapped her fingers, remembering. "Sheila said she needed to go to church more. That was it. She was bad. She done bad things," said the Righteous Puddin.

"Such as?"

"She dates lots of men!" Puddin made a face. Apparently her life with Dusty hadn't made her the biggest fan of men, in general.

Myrtle frowned. "*Lots* of men?"

"Well, a couple. That's lots in a town like Bradley."

Myrtle sighed. She was striking out here with Puddin, too. When was her luck going to turn with this case?

That night, Myrtle felt antsy. She double-checked that her door and all the windows were locked. She put Wanda's pepper spray next to her bed again. She lay down in bed only because that's what you're supposed to do at midnight...but the sleep didn't come.

At three o'clock, there was a tap at her front door and Myrtle nearly jumped through the ceiling. But murderers and other intruders didn't ever announce their presence, did they? She snatched her pepper spray off the bedside table and, gripping it in one hand and her cane threateningly in the other, she moved toward the door.

"Who's there?" she yelled in a sharp voice.

A muffled voice said with a bit of exasperation, "It's Miles."

She put down the pepper spray and cane to open the door quickly. Sure enough, there was a dark, Miles-shaped figure on her porch. And he was holding a bundle. Myrtle peered down. "What's that?" She caught her breath. "Is that...?"

She reached out to turn on the porch light and saw a pitiful Pasha, bound in a blanket. "Myowww," said the cat when it saw her.

Chapter Fourteen

"Miles! You found her!" Myrtle reached out to give Miles a hug, smashing a protesting Pasha in the process. "Here, come inside." She took the bundle from Miles's arms, crooning to it.

Miles brushed off some of the cat fur that had gotten on his clothes. "I'd be careful, Myrtle. She's scared. And she's fully armed with claws, you know."

"Poor Pasha," said Myrtle. She gently set down the bundle on the sofa and watched as Pasha fairly exploded from the covering, restlessly stalking around the room, stopping to sniff the furniture and Myrtle from time to time before finally settling down enough to sit on the floor and start grooming herself.

"However did you find her, Miles?" asked Myrtle, hurrying into the kitchen to pull out a can of tuna from her cabinet.

"I thought it through," said Miles. "Oh, and she's probably not going to want any tuna, although you can check and see."

"What do you mean, you thought it through?" asked Myrtle. She opened the can and put some on a paper plate. Pasha looked interested, so she put the plate down on the floor and watched as Pasha did a fine impression of a hungry cat.

Miles gazed thoughtfully at Pasha. "Maybe she's trying to make up for lost calories." He took off his glasses, cleaning them with his button-down shirt and then carefully putting them back on his face. "I'd read up on lost cats and their usual hiding places. They favor going under porches, under grills that are covered by tarps, under cars, behind those roll-out garbage bins...places like that. Apparently, they can hole up for long periods of time. Sometimes thirst drives them out. So I put out some old plastic containers with water in some likely spots."

Myrtle smiled down at Pasha as she quickly eliminated the tuna.

"When I saw which bowls were empty, I put a little smoked salmon at those stations later on," said Miles in his best scientific voice.

"Smoked salmon! Miles, that's horribly expensive. And you were likely feeding the town of Bradley's population of possums, raccoons, and squirrels."

"Possums and squirrels eat smoked salmon?" Miles raised his eyebrows at this.

"If they're hungry, why not? But go on, tell me more."

"Well, the smoked salmon kept disappearing at one particular location. It was a few blocks away from here, heading away from downtown. So I decided to hide down there after I set out the salmon. I had a blanket with me, so I could throw it over the cat and roll her up in it to transport her carefully here." He took off his glasses again and rubbed at what Myrtle suspected was a microscopic smudge.

"Or perhaps to prevent her from clawing you up?" asked Myrtle cannily.

"Perhaps. As I mentioned, she *is* fully armed."

Myrtle said in a wondering voice, "And you sat out in the dark like a burglar, waiting for a cat to show up?"

Miles cleared his throat. "I did actually tell the surrounding neighbors what I was doing. And Red. The neighbors I spoke with had seen the flyers, as a matter of fact. After all, I didn't think it would serve my purposes to be arrested for trespassing while I waited. Old Mrs. Adams even brought me a decaf coffee and a cookie. And a plastic yard chair to wait it out." Miles smiled. "It wasn't such a terrible experience. And now you've got Pasha."

Pasha was now licking her paw to clean the last vestiges of tuna off her face and whiskers.

"I still can't believe you shelled out that kind of money to find Pasha," mumbled Myrtle. "That must have cost...I can't even imagine. And to put food out it all over town like that."

"About twenty-five dollars for a packet of it," said Miles. He shrugged. "It was the only thing I could think of that might be a real treat for a cat—that she might really linger for."

"You don't even like Pasha, though. Pasha scratches you and hisses at you." Pasha immediately negated Myrtle's statements by trotting over to Miles and rubbing against his pants leg. He reached down and cautiously rubbed her back. Myrtle shook her head. "You don't even like her, but you did this for Pasha."

"I did this for *you*," said Miles sternly. "Because you're my friend. And you were worried."

Myrtle felt an unusual prickling in her eyes. To hide it, she said brusquely, "Thank you, Miles." And, surprising even herself, she reached over to give him a grateful hug.

Blinking furiously, Myrtle said, "Cookies? In celebration. And let's forego the milk for wine."

"You have wine here?" asked Miles in surprise.

"Hmm. Well, let's see. I keep meaning to buy some at the store, you know. But when I get to the store I remember all the other things I need and forget the wine." She peered in her fridge. "Oh. I guess I don't have wine. But I do have sherry!" She frowned. "Although it seems a little bit more of an important occasion we're celebrating than cheap sherry calls for."

Miles smiled at her. "I've actually got a very nice bottle of chardonnay at home. I'll go get it. And then I really do want to hear all the news on the case. I think I have some catching up to do."

When Miles returned with the wine, Myrtle told him all about discovering Rose's body and the talks she'd had with Claudia, Maxine and Lena. Miles listened attentively, asking a question every now and then while sipping his wine.

When she got to the part where the intruder had tried to break in, Miles sat straight up in his chair. "Did you tell Red this?" he asked her urgently. "Myrtle, that's really scary."

"What point would there be in telling Red?" she asked. "Red would simply shut me down. And I must be getting closer to the truth, since I have a murderer trying to get at me. No, Red would insist on my having a sleepover at his house and staying put there until the case is all wrapped up. But at the speed he and the state police move with these investigations, I'd be trapped over there for a month or more." She made a face. "Or worse, he'd get me locked away at Greener Pastures. He had the gall to put me on their waiting list."

"So you chased the intruder off with your pepper spray bottle," Miles said. He shook his head. ""And I'm not at all surprised to hear about the waiting list. I figured something had happened to make you mad at Red. I did notice the gnome battalion in your front yard."

"Remember how Wanda was so adamant about giving the pepper spray to me? She knew it would be helpful. I believed her, too, which is why I had the thing right next to me at night. It was in my pocketbook, although I should have had it on my bedside table. Wanda knows her forecasting, I tell you what. I know you think it's all hooey, but there you go." Myrtle took a good-sized swallow of her Chardonnay.

"Forecasting? You make it sound as if Wanda is a meteorologist." Miles smiled at the thought of Wanda in a newsroom pointing out high-pressure fronts with an emaciated arm and a nicotine-stained finger. "What else did Wanda carry on about that day? Some cryptic statement or other, wasn't it?"

"The keys are in the van," intoned Myrtle. "Who knows what that means? I guess I'll find out one day."

"So who are you thinking might be the most likely suspect now?" asked Miles. "And what do you think Rose's scribblings on the crossword mean?"

Myrtle stood up and walked over to her desk. She said, "You know, you were so successful with your careful deductions and scientific approach to finding Pasha that maybe I need to adopt some of your methods." She picked up a notebook and a pencil and sat back in her chair again.

"So now we've got Rose as a victim. I still say that the only reason someone would kill Rose is that she knew something that the killer didn't want made public." Myrtle tapped the pencil against her mouth. "Unless it's the fact that she's just generally annoying. But surely no one would murder her for that." She put Rose and Naomi's names at the top of the page and drew lines out from them.

She continued on, "Suspects would be Claudia Brown, Maxine Tristan, and Lena Fowler. I hate to take Rose off this list. She was a perfect suspect and vocal in her dislike for the victim." Myrtle pursed her lips. "But I suppose the fact that she's dead knocks her off the list." She wrote in the suspects below the victims' names.

Miles finished his wine and patted his mouth carefully with a napkin. "Couldn't she still stay on the list as a suspect in Naomi's death? It would only mean that someone else killed Rose for a separate reason."

"Welllll...I don't know. Because, as I said before, I can't honestly think of a good reason for someone to want to kill Rose. She didn't have a lot of money. She kept to herself for the most part. I think she knew something and approached the murderer about it—either to give them the chance to turn themselves in before she did, or to try to extort a bit of money from them. That's what her housekeeper thought—that she was some sort of small-time blackmailer to keep her household accounts solvent." Pasha jumped unexpectedly into Myrtle's lap and Myrtle ran her hand over her thin back. The poor cat really had gotten dependent on her for food.

Miles frowned. "I must have missed that part. About the housekeeper."

"I was talking to Puddin and she was making at least a little sense. She told me that her friend, Sheila, who'd cleaned for Rose, had thought Rose might have been trying to put pressure on someone. Sheila was indignant because she's apparently morally unimpeachable."

"Okay. So we've got Claudia, Lena, and Maxine. It sounds as if they all have motive, means, and opportunity. Or at least, they don't have alibis. I'm thinking Lena," said Miles thoughtfully.

"Why?"

"She seems very high-strung. She's obviously still reeling from being betrayed by her husband and then his unexpected death. Lena needed a scapegoat and she picked Naomi. Case closed." Miles looked very satisfied with his verdict.

"Makes sense. Except it wasn't really a *betrayal*, you know. Lena's husband wasn't having an affair with Naomi Pelter. He just made a foolish decision to climb up onto her roof."

"Either way. She's definitely angry, even if it was all fairly innocent," said Miles. "Tell me who you're favoring now?"

Myrtle said, "I don't know. Looking at this chart with all the suspects, I go back and forth. Maxine had plenty of reasons to murder Naomi. And I don't think she'd really think twice about it. There's a very cool, clinical side to her. Then there's Claudia. She's pitiful, she really is. But she had her one joy and talent in life usurped by Naomi. It seems like a good enough reason for murder to me. The only thing about Claudia is that she's so...meek. It's hard to picture her having the gumption to poison Naomi or whack Rose with a poker."

"But one of those women must have done it. Unless we think it's someone else?"

"No. No one else. These women were in garden club and attended the specific meeting and luncheon that talked about Destroying Angel mushrooms, and that would have offered an opportunity to tamper with Naomi's food," said Myrtle.

"And the cryptic crossword message? You think Rose saw some place card tampering at the garden club luncheon?" Miles raised his eyebrows. "Skullduggery at garden club?"

"That's exactly what I think. I'm going to put a little question out to the side of my diagram—*who sat next to Naomi Pelter at garden club luncheon?* Because the question I was asking before, *did you see anyone tamper with the place cards*, didn't seem to get any real answers."

"So how do you think the killer did it? Wouldn't it have been incredibly obvious if someone tampered with Naomi's food in front of everyone?" asked Miles. Pasha gave a huge yawn from Myrtle's lap and Miles gazed warily at her fangs.

"I need to find out more about that luncheon," mused Myrtle. "Maybe there was a distraction of some kind and the killer was able to easily put the sliced mushrooms on Naomi's plate without anyone watching. The salads are usually sitting on the tables when we come in for the luncheon, anyway. So there would have been time."

"How would the murderer have even known there would be mushrooms served?" asked Miles. He frowned. "That seems incredibly lucky for the killer."

Myrtle said, "No, we always know the menu in advance. Some people have food allergies and intolerances and other weird stuff and want to bring their own food. If they email it to us in advance, then vegetarian Mable knows she needs to bring her own entrée and gluten-free Clarissa knows that she'll bring corn muffins for her bread because they're serving biscuits. Everyone in that club has incredibly delicate stomachs for some reason. So the killer would easily have seen mushrooms on the menu."

Myrtle stifled a yawn and Miles said, "I think that's my cue. It sounds as if you haven't slept the last couple of nights."

Myrtle picked up Pasha and escorted Miles to the door. He turned to look at the cat, reaching out a tentative hand to pet her again. "Does this mean that Pasha is going to be an inside cat now?"

Myrtle said, "Pasha and I will have to figure that out, I suppose. Pasha is feral, so I don't even know if that's possible. I think she'll miss the outside. But I plan on keeping her in as much as possible. And if I see or hear those mean dogs again, I'm calling Red on the phone and getting him to arrest those owners. It's the owners who are at fault, not the dogs."

Maybe Pasha, now that she had a full stomach and was back at her home base actually *wanted* to resume her outdoor adventures. But Myrtle was very gratified that she decided instead to curl up at the foot of Myrtle's bed and sleep the rest of the night with her.

Chapter Fifteen

Pasha appeared content to stay inside the next morning. Myrtle fixed her a can of cat food, made sure her litter box was clean, and left her curled up on an afghan on her sofa. She'd wanted to let Red and Elaine know that Pasha was home safely. And perhaps encourage Red to pull down any flyers he saw around Bradley while he was making his rounds. After all, he'd be driving around anyway and what else did he have to do? It would be annoying to have people call her with Pasha sightings when Pasha was completely safe at home.

Myrtle found that Red had already left for the police station that day, but Elaine was home, busily cross-stitching as Jack played. It was good to see that Jack was back to his normal, happy self again. It was certainly a lot easier to be a doting grandmother when your grandchild had a sunny disposition.

"Pasha is home!" announced Myrtle, beaming.

"That's wonderful!" said Elaine with a happy gasp. She hugged Myrtle tightly and Jack came over to hug Myrtle's leg, simply because he liked hugs.

Elaine sat back down on the sofa and Myrtle sat down next to her. "Myrtle, I'm so glad! I know you've been worried sick about her. Does she look all right? Did someone find her? Or did she just come scratching on your door?"

Myrtle colored a little. "She does look all right. And, as a matter of fact, Miles found her."

"Miles?"

So Myrtle told Elaine the whole story.

"So y'all are friends again?" asked Elaine with a smile.

"Friends. Of course we *were* friends, even when we were mad—but we're friends who are *speaking* to each other again, which is much nicer. I have to hand it to Miles—his methodical nature, although it sometimes drives me crazy, actually helped to find Pasha."

"I'm just so, so glad," said Elaine with a relieved sigh. She picked up a square of cloth, pulled a needle out from where she'd tucked it into the square, and started diligently making stitches.

"How is the cross-stitching going?" asked Myrtle a bit warily. Elaine kept trying to find her true passion through various crafts. Judging by the results, she hadn't hit on it yet.

"Great!" said Elaine brightly. She brought the cross-stitch over for Myrtle to see. It was a pattern of a little owl sitting on a branch, looking wise.

Myrtle could tell that the owl's head was much bigger on one side than it was on the other. What's more, Elaine appeared to continue making *x*s on that lopsided part of the owl's head. Elaine seemed to be waiting for her to say something about her artwork. Myrtle cleared her throat. "How cute! Yes. Very cute. Ahh...good job."

She was relieved to see that Elaine was taking the warped owl away again and was now putting it on a nearby table. A cloud passed over Elaine's face and Myrtle frowned. Had her initial reaction to the owl been obvious?

But soon it became clear that Elaine had something else on her mind. "I'm glad you came by today, Myrtle—especially since Red isn't around this morning. There was something that was weighing on me a little and I thought you should know."

"That sounds serious," said Myrtle. "What is it? Nothing with your health, is it? Or Jack's or Red's?" Or the little owl's, since he clearly had a tumor on the side of his head?

"Nooo, no. Nothing like that, Myrtle. Rest assured." Elaine glanced away from Myrtle and seemed to be choosing her words with care. "Now promise me you won't let Red know I talked to you, because you know I don't want to get in the middle of any arguments between the two of you. I love both of you. Very, very much."

"For Pete's sake, Elaine! Spit it out!"

Elaine said, "Okay. Red arranged for a representative from Greener Pastures Retirement Home to pick you up and take you on a tour of the facility. They're taking a couple of other ladies from Bradley, too, apparently."

"What?" Myrtle felt a burning rush of a white-hot anger that threatened to completely undo her.

Elaine grimaced. "I know. It's the last thing you want and you've been very vocal about it. If it helps at all, I can tell you that Red genuinely believes that the move would be good for you—that you'd be safer there and would enjoy yourself more than you think."

"Well, it's good to know that Red is completely deluded. Remind me to tear up my health care power of attorney. My health and general welfare certainly don't need to be in *his* hands. Perhaps he has early-onset dementia." Myrtle struggled to keep her temper in check. Elaine didn't deserve to be at the receiving end of it, after all. And Jack was already staring curiously at her.

"Thanks for letting me know, Elaine," she said in a warm voice without the snippiness she'd used earlier. "I appreciate it. I'll figure out how to handle this and Red won't know that you said a thing about it."

Myrtle had a feeling that "handling it" meant that as soon as she saw a car from Greener Pastures out front, she was going to be slipping out the back door.

Elaine seemed ready to change the subject. "I'm glad you're all right after discovering poor Rose yesterday. I know you seemed fine when I took you to Lena Fowler's, but I thought maybe you would have had nightmares all last night."

"It was certainly a shock yesterday morning. Especially after finding Naomi in the same spot during the book club meeting. It's been a very peculiar week."

"I still can't imagine who would do such a thing," said Elaine, resuming her cross-stitching and passionately adding more *x*s to the side of the owl's head.

"Everyone I've spoken with seems very surprised. And apparently no one has seen Rose out and about the last couple of days—I guess having Naomi expire in her living room was more taxing on her than she'd admitted," said Myrtle. Jack brought her an airplane and she beamed at him as she made airplane noises and had it "fly" around her.

"To me, it sounds as if everyone is lying," said Elaine with a short laugh. I've seen Rose out a couple of times, myself. And

I saw her chatting with Claudia outside in her yard yesterday morning."

"What?" Myrtle stopped flying the airplane around to stare at Elaine.

"Sure. The weather has been so hot that I haven't been able to exercise in the afternoons. Plus, the only time I can leave to exercise during the week is early in the morning with Red gone. I've been trying to walk very early a few times a week."

"How early?"

"Well, not as early as *you* walk around. Not at four in the morning or three in the morning," said Elaine with a snort. "But I'm out there right before seven. I've seen Claudia chat with Rose before yesterday, as a matter of fact, on my walks. Claudia tries to walk then, too, and Rose was very, very predictable about the time she'd go get her newspaper."

Why hadn't Claudia said she'd seen Rose? Myrtle frowned and absently handed the plane back to Jack who took off running with it.

A key rattled in the front door and Red came through, greeting them and swinging Jack through the air when he ran toward him. Elaine gave Myrtle a concerned look, knowing that Red wasn't exactly in Myrtle's good graces with the whole Greener Pastures thing. Myrtle gave Elaine a reassuring wink. She certainly wasn't going to give everything away and tattle on her informant. Myrtle would put up a show of tolerating Red. Temporarily.

So she said to Red, "I was just telling Elaine that Miles brought Pasha back to me last night. He'd set up a sort of trap for her. Not *really* a trap. I guess he simply lured her to a particular spot and then threw a blanket over her. She seems like she's skinny and a little dirty, but none the worse for her adventure."

Red grinned. "Really? Well, that's fantastic news, Mama. It really is. So you and Miles are friendly again, are you?"

Red appeared to be missing the point of the good news. The good news wasn't that she and Miles had made up—it was that Pasha was back. She gritted her teeth and decided to continue acting as if Red wasn't irritating the stew out of her. "Yes, that's right. And it's great to have the cat back home, too."

Elaine gave a relieved sigh that Myrtle clearly was keeping a lid on her emotions.

Myrtle gave Red a very pleasant smile. "Which reminds me. While you're doing your rounds in Bradley, could you take off the different posters and flyers that you see posted around town?"

Myrtle reflected on her visit as she walked back across the street to her home. So Claudia wasn't telling the truth, then, about not having seen Rose since book club. That was Myrtle's takeaway from her conversation with Elaine. Well, that and Red's total and complete perfidy.

She opened her front door and saw Pasha sleeping, curled in a sunbeam on the living room floor. Pasha raised her head briefly to see Myrtle, and then lay back down for more napping. The poor cat must be exhausted from her terrifying adventure.

Myrtle headed to the kitchen to make lunch. She could catch up on some of her soap opera while she ate. Things moved so fast on *Tomorrow's Promise* that if she didn't watch for a couple of days, babies could suddenly be preschoolers and sweet teenagers could end up as shoplifting drug dealers. Myrtle made a tomato sandwich and plopped down in front of the television.

As she feared, Angelique, who'd been a darling character—a Sunday school teaching, literacy-volunteering soccer mom—had suddenly morphed into a trashy vixen. She'd thought she'd pulled up the most recent missed episode but clearly Myrtle had either missed a storyline in a previous show or else she'd hit play on the wrong date.

Angelique was actually acting a lot like Naomi or Maxine. She sort of looked like them, too—heavily made-up, lots of teeth, and that flattering, flirty manner. Myrtle started thinking about the competition between Maxine and Naomi. It was true that the town of Bradley was not exactly comprised of a ton of eligible bachelors. But, on the other hand, it wasn't full of eligible single women, either. Most of the single women were like Myrtle...or Erma next door, thought Myrtle with a shudder.

There was a knock at Myrtle's door. Pasha lifted her head and made a low growl. "It's okay, Pasha," said Myrtle. She hit pause on the show to save her place, found her cane, and hurried to the door. She peered out the side window.

It was Claudia. She looked frazzled. "Miss Myrtle, I was supposed to give you something for book club when I saw you and I forgot completely. I guess I forgot because of all the talk about Rose." She gulped as if the name were hard to get out. "Anyway, you might have missed this because we talked about it during a meeting that you missed, but I'm the new secretary for book club." Her eyes brightened a bit as she disclosed her new, executive position in the club.

Did book club even have a secretary? Had Myrtle just missed that fact for the last million years? She knew it had a president. It was certainly a sign of her book club's incompetence that they had chosen poor Claudia as secretary.

"We're doing something a little different for the next meeting. Since the last meeting had...well, had something very sad happen. And since we didn't get any business actually accomplished at the last meeting because of...the incident, we're going to go ahead and have a meeting instead of waiting for another month. We're going to talk about some of our favorite books and then we're going to place a bid for a chance to choose the next book club title." Claudia's eyes shone behind her cat eye glasses.

"What...an auction? To choose next month's pick?" asked Myrtle. She would love to pick *The Sound and the Fury*. She would even pay for the pleasure of seeing everyone's jaws drop to the floor when she announced the selection. But really—what good was a book club in the South that never read Faulkner? The only problem with that was that she had no money on this sad little fixed income of hers. Perhaps she could blackmail someone into putting money in on that title. Hmm.

Claudia said, "That's right. And then the money that we raise goes to charity in memory of Naomi and Rose."

"A charity? What kind of charity?"

"Oh, well, I thought maybe animals. Since they loved animals so much. You know—the flyers for the missing cat and all."

Myrtle had known Claudia was spacy, but this brought spacy to a new height. "Claudia, you know those are *my* flyers? Remember, I was the one who was had the missing cat."

"Right. Right. Oh, you're right, I'm so sorry." Claudia's face was crestfallen. "Sometimes I don't pay attention very well. I guess something like a nature conservancy or something, then? Since they loved nature."

"Did they? As I recall, Naomi's death was directly related to nature. In the form of a mushroom, actually. Now *Rose*, on the other hand...yes, she was probably more of a fan of nature in general. But I've got to applaud you on the overall idea—it's a very nice way to handle this sensitive topic. Book club has certainly endured more than its fair share of loss lately. When is this next meeting?"

Claudia reddened. "Tomorrow, actually."

"*Tomorrow?*"

"I kept forgetting to tell you," said Claudia miserably.

"But you told everyone else?"

"Yes. Well, I sent them an email."

"You didn't send *me* an email?" Myrtle narrowed her eyes.

"Well, no. I figured you didn't have a computer." Claudia was actually wringing her hands. Myrtle didn't think she'd ever seen anyone who really did that. Wasn't that something only done in books?

Myrtle stepped back and waved her arm with a flourish to reveal her desk with her very nice computer and printer. "I blog, Claudia. For the newspaper. I promise you I'm quite adept at the computer."

"Oh. I just thought...with your age and everything—you know." Claudia blinked at the computer and printer.

"I am most certainly very old. But I haven't lost my marbles. And I enjoy learning new things. So please include me on your email list." Myrtle turned, jotted down her email address on a sticky note and handed it to Claudia. "It's all right—you wouldn't have known," said Myrtle with more kindness than she actually felt.

Claudia was recovering somewhat. "I sure will, Miss Myrtle. Wow. Blogging. I think you might be better on a computer than I am."

"Before you go, Claudia, I did have one more thing that I wanted to ask you about. I know you told me during our conversation yesterday that you hadn't seen Rose since book club, but I spoke with someone this morning who mentioned seeing you talking to Rose on the morning she died." Myrtle said this in what she considered a very non-accusatory voice. The last thing she wanted was for Claudia to crumble in front of her like she did before.

Claudia still fell apart. Apparently, she was more fragile than Myrtle had imagined.

Her eyes flooded with tears. "Oh, Miss Myrtle. I was so worried about what people might say. I didn't want to be a suspect in Rose's death like I was for Naomi's. I knew the police were thinking I might have had something to do with Naomi and if I told you or them that I saw Rose that morning—what might they think?"

They might think she did it. Myrtle's mind was going in that direction, herself. "But it's foolish to lie, Claudia. Lies are so easy to get found out—especially in small towns like Bradley. Everybody knows everybody. Everybody knows everyone's routines. So you used to talk to Rose when she was out getting her paper, right? That's when you'd take a little walk?"

Claudia nodded and looked down at the floor. "The doctor told me that I should try to exercise in the mornings before it got hot outside. That had been my excuse, you know—that it was too hot to walk and that was the only exercise I liked to do."

"Did Rose say anything to you when you were talking to her?" asked Myrtle intently.

Claudia knit her brows in confusion. "She talked, yes. It would have been rude for her not to."

Myrtle took a deep breath. "I mean—did she say anything important? Did she mention that she was expecting company that morning, for instance? Or that she was worried about anything?"

"I don't think Rose was ever worried about anything. She fussed about things, she didn't worry about them."

Fair enough. And probably very true.

"I think," said Myrtle in her very best Stern Schoolteacher Voice, "that we are dealing with someone very dangerous here. I wonder if the person responsible for murdering Naomi and Rose is afraid—and is trying to cover her tracks by considering killing others. I had someone try to break into my home the other night and I believe it's because I'm asking questions."

Claudia's eyes were huge behind her cat eye glasses.

"Can you think of *anything* at the garden club luncheon that was odd? Did you see anyone replacing food on Naomi Pelter's plate?" asked Myrtle.

Claudia frowned in thought for a moment, and then shook her head reluctantly.

"Can you remember who sat next to Naomi at the luncheon?"

Claudia looked a bit panicked. "My memory is so awful. I have to sit down to think."

Myrtle realized she'd never offered Claudia a seat. "I'm sorry—of course you should sit down."

Claudia plopped down abruptly into an armchair and pressed her fingers hard into her temples as if to force out the memories. The look on her face resembled someone with a fatal migraine. Then her face brightened. "I do! I do remember who sat next to Naomi."

"Who?"

"It was Erma! You know—Erma Sherman." Claudia looked like a puppy waiting eagerly for positive reinforcement in the form of a treat.

"Good job, Claudia," said Myrtle. Erma? She was an abhorrent neighbor, an abysmal gardener, a repulsive conversationalist. She drove too fast, laughed too loud, and had bad breath. But Erma was no murderer. Of that, Myrtle was convinced.

"Thinking back, Claudia—since you did such a good job remembering that seating arrangement—can you think who might have been on Naomi's *other* side?"

Claudia's face clouded. "Her other side?"

"Yes. Wasn't there someone sitting on the other side of Naomi?"

"I—don't remember." Now Claudia was dejected again.

"No worries! No worries, Claudia. I'm sure I can find out who might have sat there." From Erma. Shoot. After weeks of avoiding Erma like a particularly contagious and undesirable disease, now she'd be chasing her down to figure out what she might know.

"Well, thanks for letting me know about book club. And do add me to your email list," said Myrtle. Claudia still sat, looking at her. Myrtle cleared her throat. "Don't let me keep you, my dear. I know you're very busy. Doing...?" She raised her eyebrows, inviting Claudia to fill in the blanks.

"Oh! Yes. What time is it? I've got to work on the book selection auction for tomorrow. I'd better run. Thanks, Miss Myrtle." Claudia hurriedly stood up and rushed to the door.

Myrtle noticed as she walked back to watch the rest of her soap that Claudia had forgotten the piece of paper with Myrtle's email address on it. Pooh.

Chapter Sixteen

"Miles, how much money do you have?" asked Myrtle. She'd called him up just as soon as her soap was over. In fact, she'd found her mind wandering a bit during the soap opera, planning her next move.

"How much *money* do I have? Now that's a pretty personal question, isn't it, Myrtle?" Miles's voice was slightly indignant.

"No, no, I mean how much money can you *spare*? If I asked you to sponsor me in something?" asked Myrtle.

"Sponsor you? For what? Myrtle, you're not planning on signing up for that marathon I was reading about, are you?"

"Marathon? For heaven's sake, Miles. Have you been drinking? I'm in my eighties. The only time you're going to catch me running is if something really scary is chasing me. Even then, I'll probably just give in."

"Oh. Then this might have something to do with the book club meeting tomorrow, right?" Miles sounded wary now. "The auction?"

"Yes. How did you find out about it, by the way? Did Claudia tell you about it?" asked Myrtle. Was she the *only* one who didn't get an email?

"Tell me about it? Well, she emailed me, of course."

Myrtle gritted her teeth. But considering that she needed Miles, she decided that this time she was going to just shrug off her irritation. "Okay. Yes, it's about the auction. You know how we've been trying to take over book club for ages? A coup to convert the group to literary fiction or classical literature?"

"I know that *you've* been trying to take over book club with a coup," corrected Miles, with heavy emphasis on the replacement pronoun.

"I thought this might be just as good of a means to an end. So we'll be the highest bidder for the opportunity to pick the selection. You know this is the only way, Miles. Every meeting, book club selections are proposed. I always suggest an amazing title. Then we put it up to a vote with a show of hands. And my picks are never chosen. Never!" Myrtle spat the words out into the phone.

"Won't the bidding go super-high if they see that you're putting in a selection, Myrtle? I'm not sure how much money I want to devote to this scheme. What book are you planning to propose?"

Myrtle smiled to herself. This was the *pièce de résistance*. She knew that Miles was really going to come onboard as soon as he heard this particular author and title. "Oh, I thought I'd choose some good old Southern literature. From our friend William Faulkner. *The Sound and the Fury.*"

She heard the indrawn breath on the other end of the phone and smiled again.

"Well, at least you've picked something I can stand behind. All right, I'm in. But I don't want to lose my shirt in this auction,

Myrtle. I know the proceeds go to charity, but I *am* on a fixed income, you know."

Myrtle rolled her eyes. Miles may be on a retirement income, but she had the strong impression that he had plenty in the bank to draw on. "It's a silent auction, Miles. And the bidding *won't* go high because they won't see me filling out a card—they'll only see *you* filling out an auction card. That's the real beauty of the plan. And I'm sure, once they read a little Faulkner, that he will have a transforming effect on our club. We'll finally be able to ditch all those books with titles like *Jennifer's Promise* and end up reading some real books."

"All right," said Miles shortly. "I'll see you tomorrow at the book club then. And I'll take care of the book selection."

"You'll *see* me there, but don't hang out with me, all right? People might get suspicious that you and I are planning together. Besides, I'm going to be talking with Erma Sherman at the book club meeting."

There was silence on the other end of the phone. Then Miles said suspiciously, "Myrtle, have you had a small stroke?"

Myrtle snorted. "As if. I know it sounds strange, but I need to talk to Erma about the case. Claudia told me that Erma was sitting next to Naomi at the garden club luncheon."

"You don't think *Erma* killed Naomi Pelter? Because if that's where you're going with this, I couldn't agree less. Erma is very annoying, of course, but ...."

"Yes, I know. She's annoying but she doesn't kill people. She might kill them with boredom, but not in a literal sense. The thing about Erma, though, is that she has an excellent memory. It's the one remarkable thing about her. And she has no discretion at all—she'll be happy to spill the beans on whatever she saw at the garden club luncheon the day that Naomi ended up with poisonous mushrooms on her plate. The only problem will be sifting through all the garbage that Erma will spew out for the actual helpful information." Myrtle's head started throbbing on cue as she considered this issue.

"But why ask Erma at book club? She lives right next door. Just hop over right now."

Myrtle shuddered. "No. If I visit Erma now, I'll get trapped over there and will never get away. She'll start talking about her bunions and the odd mole she had taken off the side of her nose. If I talk to her at book club, it will be more of a controlled environment and I can get away from her. You can help with that, as a matter of fact. If you see me looking desperate, you can rescue me from Erma."

"You always look desperate when you're talking with Erma, though. How will I know if it's time to interrupt or not?" asked Miles.

"How about if I scratch my head? That can be our signal. Then you can come over with some sort of manufactured excuse and help me make my escape. As long as it's after the silent auction! I can't be seen colluding with you before it."

There was a deep sigh on Miles's side of the phone.

Book club was actually being hosted by Maxine this time and everyone was asked to bring a covered dish. Elaine dropped Myrtle off and then left to run errands. Myrtle wielded a large dip and chip container in one hand and her cane in the other. Maxine hastily relieved Myrtle of the serving dish and greeted Myrtle with a smile. "Are you ready for our little auction, Miss

Myrtle? Knowing you, I thought you might be itching to get at the table with the bidding cards."

Myrtle was dismayed to feel her cheeks color. "Oh. No, Maxine, I figured I'd let the young people have at it this time. You know. Let them take a stab at picking the book. I'm on a fixed income. A retired teacher. Can't be flinging money into something like this."

Maxine gave her an amused smile. "Miss Myrtle, it would give me great joy to sponsor you. I don't have a lot of extra income either, but it'd be worth it to see the look on the others' faces when we end up having to read *The Pilgrim's Progress* or something."

As tempting as it sounded, Myrtle resisted the urge to collaborate with Maxine on the auction. Who knew if Maxine could even keep a secret? Besides, if anyone saw her even approaching the table to make a bid, she bet the amounts of the bids would grow by fifty percent or more just to try to shut Myrtle down.

"No, it's all right. Really. Thanks, though."

Maxine lifted a well-shaped eyebrow in surprise at Myrtle's meek tone. "All right, then. Whichever way you want it. Oh, and I decided to inject book club with a little pizazz today, since we're doing something different with the auction and all. I've put out some specialty drinks. Some tea."

Myrtle leveled a look at her. "Tea. Mm-hm. We have tea every single book club meeting and have done since the 1920s, according to the book club's original bylaws. So what's in this tea that makes it a specialty drink?"

"Technically, it's a Long Island Iced Tea." Maxine smiled as Myrtle showed recognition of the drink. "So you're not just a sherry drinker, then?"

"I'm not much of a drinker, although I have tasted that particular drink before. I believe I was told it had vodka, gin, tequila, and rum in it, along with a mixer. As I recall, it was incredibly potent, but didn't taste as if it had alcohol in it at all." Myrtle thoughtfully gazed at Maxine.

"This one has a little triple-sec in it, too. And therein lies the fun," said Maxine smugly. "I figured book club could use some lightening up."

"So I'm guessing you didn't inform your victims of the contents of the tea?" Myrtle gave her a stern, schoolteacher look.

"Only a couple of choice candidates. Like yourself. I'm not planning on drinking, myself, so I'll drive everyone home who needs a ride. Shoot, Miss Myrtle, most of the members can walk home in less than a couple of minutes." Maxine gave a rueful sigh. "Why do I feel as if you're going to give me after-school detention?"

"It's really not any of my business what you choose to do at your party," said Myrtle. "I just hope your carpets or car won't need cleaning after the meeting. I foresee some book club members might toss their cookies."

Book club did indeed seem rather lively as Myrtle entered Maxine's house. There seemed to be a lot more laughter than there usually was. Loud laughter. She spotted Miles right away and noted that, sure enough, he did have a glass in his hand and had consumed most of what was in the glass. Unlike the other guests, however, he wasn't being raucous or laughing loudly. He was very solemnly sitting in a corner of the room. Apparently, alcohol must have made him reflective.

Erma tottered over to Myrtle right away. Unfortunately, it appeared that she became even more obnoxious when she drank. "Myrtle, you've got to have some of this tea. Isss del-ishus!" She mangled the word *delicious* and thrust her cup out for Myrtle to taste the tea.

Myrtle put a hand out to block the glass. "No thanks, Erma. I'm not very thirsty right now."

Erma swayed a bit on her feet and took another sip herself. "Are you going to put in a bid for the silent auction?" she asked. "We all guessed that you were going to write down *War and Peace* or something. We were going to put in big bids, if you did!"

Which was exactly why Myrtle wasn't going anywhere near that table. She glanced over thoughtfully at Miles who looked a little bleary. He gave her a small thumbs-up sign, which she took to mean that he'd already sneaked in a bid for *The Sound and the Fury*.

Several other book club members joined them, including Maxine, who smirked at Myrtle as she observed her handiwork in the swaying members. Maxine was going to have to rent a van to get all these folks home.

"No," said Myrtle with a gracious smile, "I'm not planning on putting in a bid for the book selection. Not that I don't think animal rights is a good cause."

Claudia Brown hiccupped near her elbow. "Not animal rights. No. It's...." She looked around to the others for help.

Erma stepped in again. "The bird society. Right? Audubon?"

Claudia shrugged. "Something like that."

Myrtle said, "Nothing against Audubon, then. But I'm a retired schoolteacher, you know." She drew herself up to her full height with great dignity and gazed down at Claudia from six feet up. "On a fixed income. There are many things that I have to cut back on and charitable giving is, sadly, one of those. I'm practically worthy of a charity, myself." She looked as pitiful as she could manage.

"Well of *course* you can't place a bid!" cried Claudia, punctuating her sentence with another hiccup. "And who can blame you?"

Tippy Chambers, weaving a bit on her heels (she was always a snappy dresser), agreed with Claudia. "We only thought that you cared so much for classical literature that you'd be sure to enter a selection."

Myrtle said graciously, "I'm sure I'll enjoy whatever pick wins the auction. And, if it's a beach book, I'll simply imagine myself on a beach as I'm reading it."

The club members all beamed at her.

Tippy said, "I think I'm going to have more of that delicious tea."

Claudia quickly said, "I'll join you."

The small group moved toward the refreshment table, but Myrtle reached out and caught Erma's arm before she could move away. "I wanted to talk to you for a minute, Erma."

Erma's ego was such that she would never question this statement, even though Myrtle had never shown any interest in talking with her, for a minute or otherwise, before. "Okay," she said, giving her sneering smile. Then she squinted, staring across the room. "Why is Miles looking at us like that? He's giving me the creeps."

Miles was still sitting quietly in the corner. He gazed solemnly at the two women, and then lifted one hand in greeting. He was smashed. Myrtle certainly hoped he had already put in a bid for the book...with any luck, before he started drinking that tea.

"I think he's just tired," said Myrtle brusquely. "Listen, Erma. This could be important."

Erma gave a big sway this time and Myrtle resisted any impulse to try to steady her. Erma was big enough to pull Myrtle to the ground with her and Myrtle didn't fancy a broken hip at this time. Erma caught herself and tried to arrange her features into a focused expression. "Okay. What is it?"

"The garden club luncheon that we just recently had...do you remember much about it?"

"You didn't go," said Erma in a loud voice. "Don't you like garden club anymore?"

Several book club members glanced in their direction.

Myrtle said in a hushed voice that she hoped Erma would replicate, "I like it fine, Erma. I've just been busy. Now, can you remember who you sat next to at the luncheon?"

"I sure can. I sat next to Naomi Pelter. She was fascinated (Erma slurred the word almost beyond recognition) when I told her all about my kidney stones. Hung on every word."

"Oh, I'm *sure* she must have." Myrtle said. "And can you recall, Erma, who was on the other *side* of Naomi?"

Erma swayed a little again and her eyes glazed a bit. "Myrtle, thinking about gardening. Have you noticed that my grass is dying near the fence? What do you make of it?"

"Oh, that crabgrass? I think it might be afflicted with that virulent crabgrass disease that I heard about on the national news. A terrible thing. You should replace it with sod."

Erma frowned. "I watch the national news, too. I didn't see any stories on crabgrass disease. I thought that crabgrass was like cockroaches—they'd be the last things in the world to die in the case of nuclear holocaust."

Erma butchered most of the words that came out of her mouth now. Myrtle felt a sense of desperation to get the information she needed before Erma was a lost cause.

"I watch PBS, Erma. The hour-long news program. And I can promise you that they spoke at great length on the tragic crabgrass disease that is sweeping our country. Now, do you remember who sat on the other side of Naomi at the garden club luncheon?" Myrtle kept her voice low and it came out with a hiss.

Erma's features brightened as she remembered. "Why, Maxine Tristan! Our hostess! She sat on the other side of Naomi at the luncheon. And she kept getting up the whole time!"

Erma's voice was booming and it carried, even in a room of loud laughter. Myrtle gave a nervous glance over her shoulder and was horrified to see Maxine standing very close. But what had she heard? Maxine's face reflected nothing.

"Do you ladies need anything else to eat or drink? Miss Myrtle, you haven't gotten anything to drink yet." Maxine gave her a smile.

"I'm not very thirsty, but thanks," said Myrtle giving her a return smile. Apparently, her conversation with Erma was over because suddenly the woman lurched out of the room in the direction of the restroom.

Maxine's eyes twinkled. "This is the best book club ever!"

"Hadn't we better get started, though? I'm worried that the members won't be able to function in another few minutes. Shouldn't we get the auction going? Has everyone placed a bid?"

Maxine gave Myrtle an amused expression. There was something else there, too, something Myrtle couldn't really put a finger on.

Maxine cleared her throat and lifted her head to call across the room, "Has everyone placed a bid in the silent auction? Everyone who was going to, that is?" She paused and everyone in the room seemed to be staring at Myrtle. Myrtle shook her head to indicate that she wasn't placing one. No one made a move toward the table.

"All right, then. In that case, as hostess, I will state that the auction is closed." Maxine clapped her hands together to emphasize her words. "Now, let's find out who had the highest bid. Unless Claudia, as our esteemed treasurer wants to?" Claudia shook her head violently. Maxine nodded, and then strode to the table and leaned over it, glancing at the bids. Everyone in the room watched her with big eyes. Claudia Brown hiccupped again.

"And the winner is...." Maxine mischievously glanced around her to raise the tension as she paused. "Miles Bradford!"

There was both applause and long faces. "No worries," called out Maxine. "I think we'll have to do this again. This was too much fun to have it be a one-off. Miles, would you like to tell us all the title for the next book club meeting? We're all waiting with bated breath."

Miles was still sitting solemnly in his spot, looking a bit sleepy. He stood up. "Um, yes. The title of the book we'll be reading for our next meeting is by William Faulkner. It's *The Sound and the Fury*."

Dead silence greeted this announcement. Myrtle smiled. A wide grin spread across Maxine's face.

Chapter Seventeen

Then everyone turned to look at Myrtle.

"What is it?" asked Myrtle innocently.

"You put Miles up to that!" said Tippy Chambers, icily.

Myrtle decided it would be wise not to definitively answer any allegations or make any defense. "Miles simply has good taste. Faulkner is a classic," she said. "He's probably one of the most famous Southern writers we've got. I'm thrilled we're going to read him in book club."

Tippy looked as if her head hurt. "I read Mr. Faulkner in college," she said slowly. "I didn't understand a word. Didn't he write in...what was it? Unconsciousness?"

"Stream of consciousness. Yes, that's his narrative style in *The Sound and the Fury*." Several book club members glared at her. "I might have read it before," Myrtle said with a small shrug. "I'm a former English teacher, y'all. I will tell you that I think you'll enjoy the stream of consciousness. It's going to show the mental workings of a character who, like Winnie the Pooh, has very little brain. And who doesn't like Pooh?"

Miles, intoxicated though he was, furrowed his brow to indicate that Myrtle's analogy was something of a stretch. But

Myrtle had the feeling that if she tried to hook the club members on the fact that the book's title came from a famous soliloquy in Shakespeare's *Macbeth*, she was going to get nowhere.

"So we're reading Pooh?" asked Claudia hopefully. "I like the idea of rereading books from my childhood."

Everyone stared at Claudia.

Tippy, struck a bit more sober by her horror of the book club selection, said, "Maxine? What *exactly* was in that iced tea?"

Maxine gave her a wolfish grin. "Whatever do you mean, Tippy?"

"You know what I mean! Look at how dippy everyone is acting. I think you spiked that tea." Tippy glowered at Maxine through narrowed eyes.

The members gave Tippy a somewhat irritated look at being called dippy.

Claudia started to howl. It was a ghastly sound, punctuated by hiccups as it was. "Oh! But I don't drink!"

Miles rubbed his temples as if he were trying to think it through. "So...we've all had quite a bit to drink."

Claudia cried louder and Myrtle rolled her eyes.

"Not *everyone*, no. But it appears as though everyone but Miss Myrtle and I have had too much."

"I thought it was the best punch ever," wailed Claudia.

"I think I know why you don't drink," said Maxine with a sigh. "Don't waste tears over something like this, Claudia. I'll get you safely home. And if you take an aspirin, drink a glass of water and have a little something to eat, then you'll be perfectly fine. I only thought to add a little pizazz to our special meeting," said Maxine innocently. "I made the teas Long Island Iced Teas in celebration."

A collective groan rose from the assembled.

"But not to worry! I will be driving home everyone who feels they need a ride. And then coming back to consume the remainder of the tea, myself." She gave a husky laugh. "Miss Myrtle doesn't appear to have drunk anything either, so she could drive some folks home in their car and then they could walk to her house later on to collect their vehicle."

There were no takers. You could hear crickets. Myrtle gritted her teeth. She was a *good* driver. And she never drove a hair over thirty-five. Discrimination against the elderly. Again.

While everyone was arranging to either walk home or have Maxine take them, Myrtle thoughtfully watched Maxine.

Only Miles took Myrtle up on her offer of a ride home. And she had a feeling that Miles had only agreed because he thought she'd be mad if he didn't. "How are you feeling?" asked Myrtle, glancing at Miles as he sat in the passenger seat. "You've been very quiet the whole time."

"Alcohol makes me sleepy," he said with a sigh. "Or, at any rate, liquor makes me sleepy. I don't have the issue with wine as much." He clutched his door with a tight grip.

Myrtle decided to graciously overlook the fact that Miles was nervous at being a passenger with her. "Well, our plan was a success, anyway. Aren't you glad about that?"

A grin spread across Miles's face. "I am. I really am. It was hard not to grin like a crazy man when Maxine announced that I had the winning bid. Faulkner! We get to read Faulkner in book club." He beamed.

"Yes, indeed, a tremendous success. A good thing, because you know we'll never be able to pull that off again. Ever. Now that they know you're on Team Myrtle, even if they *do* have another silent auction, they'll be bidding up into the stratosphere to ensure that you and I are shut down. So we'd better enjoy our Faulkner. The best we can hope for is that they see the error of their ways after they read *The Sound and the Fury* and start adding more classical literature into the mix." Myrtle carefully pulled up into Miles's driveway. "How much did you have to invest to ensure the highest bid?"

Miles looked a bit glum once again. "Fifty-five dollars."

"Well." Myrtle cleared her throat. "That's a nice donation to a worthy cause."

"Did we ever find out what the cause was?" asked Miles, looking sideways at her.

"Uh...no. No, we didn't. But I'm sure it's something good. Good causes usually are good, after all."

Miles nodded. Then he rubbed his forehead. "I'm already starting to get a headache. How ridiculous. I'd have been eating more hors d'oeuvres if I'd thought I was actually drinking." He sighed, and then glanced over at Myrtle. "So what did you find out? I saw you talking with Erma. I knew if you kept talking to her, it must mean you were getting some information. And I didn't see you scratching your head."

"Yes. She remembered very clearly, apparently. Maxine sat on Naomi's other side. Although apparently, she was out of her seat a lot. I guess she was talking with other garden club members or going to the ladies room or getting more drinks or something."

"Is that what you really think?" asked Miles, gazing at her.

Myrtle shook her head. "No, unfortunately. I rather like Maxine, but I think she was up and down and walking around so that people would have a harder time remembering that she sat there. To put some distance between herself and Naomi."

"Who would put Naomi and Maxine next to each other anyway?" grunted Miles. "I thought they couldn't stand each other."

"I think that's the point," said Myrtle slowly. "I think that's what Claudia was saying in her very vague way. Maxine re-arranged those place cards. No one in their right mind would put those two next to each other."

Miles was quiet for a few moments, taking it all in. "Why else would she want to rearrange the place cards? What other reason would she have to want to sit next to Naomi Pelter?"

Myrtle looked at him. "I can't think of any."

Miles nodded. "But of course we have no proof. So we can't call Red and tell him what you're thinking. So this seems like a good time...for a nap."

"I might even put my feet up, myself. Here, I'll leave the car here in your driveway and walk home. Got my cane right here."

Miles frowned. "Weren't you carrying something with you when you arrived at book club?"

Myrtle tilted her head to remember and then growled, "The silly dip and chip dish. I leave that thing every time I go any-where. Oh well, I guess I'll get it back later."

"Someone must have dropped you off. You wouldn't have been able to walk over there with a dip and chip dish in one hand and a cane in your other."

"Elaine did. On her way out to run errands. We figured you'd just give me a ride back. It's okay. I won't need the container until next book club anyway." Myrtle climbed out of the car and headed briskly home. "See you later," she called over her shoulder. "Be sure to drink water!"

Myrtle fed Pasha, who seemed pleased to see her. Then she decided to indulge by reading some of *The Sound and the Fury*. She just happened to have a well-worn copy beside her bed. Pasha decided to curl up next to her leg as she put her feet up to read.

She'd made it through the first fifty pages when her doorbell rang. Pasha growled and Myrtle frowned. "Who could that be? Seems like I saw everyone I knew at that book club meeting."

Pasha ran under the bed as Myrtle grabbed her cane and moved to the door. She peered out the side window and saw Maxine there. Maxine saw her and smiled and held up the dip and chip dish. Myrtle hesitated. She did think that Maxine was behind Naomi's death. But wouldn't it seem even odder if Myrtle didn't open the door? Wouldn't that make Maxine even more suspicious? After all, Maxine didn't really know she was onto her. She was going to be prepared, though. "One second, Maxine! One second." She seized her cane.

Where was her pepper spray? Myrtle's breath hissed out in an angry sigh as she checked her pocketbook and on the bedside table. Nothing. Must have laid it down somewhere. She hurried to the kitchen and grabbed a knife, instead. Then she returned to the front door.

Myrtle forced a smile and slowly unlocked the door. "Maxine," she said in as friendly a voice as she could muster. "That's awfully kind of you to bring my dish by. But you didn't have to—I could have gotten it later on." She propped her cane against the wall and held out that hand for the dish.

Maxine moved forward, "Oh, I'll bring it in, Miss Myrtle. I wanted to have a little visit."

"Now isn't a good time," said Myrtle firmly. She pushed back. "But thanks for the dish." She kept her hand stretched out for the dish.

"*I* think it's a good time," said Maxine. And the younger woman pushed her way through into the house, closing the door behind her.

Chapter Eighteen

M yrtle held out the knife in front of her and grabbed at her cane with the other. "Now that you're in here, you can make a phone call for me. Give Red a call and tell him that I've solved his murders for him and that he can collect his perp from my house."

A smile spread across Maxine's face. "Clever aren't you? But a horrible actress, Miss Myrtle. I could tell at book club that you'd found something out after you talked to Erma Sherman. It was written all over your face. But you've made the mistake of bringing a knife to a gunfight." She revealed that she'd been holding a pistol under the dip and chip dish. "Now put that knife down."

Myrtle reluctantly lowered the knife, but didn't drop it. "This is stupid, Maxine. And you're not a stupid woman. There's no way you can get away with this. Your car is out in my driveway. I live directly across the street from the police chief who is a fairly observant man and likely saw you outside on my front step with my serving dish. If I end up dead from a gunshot wound, who do you think will be the most likely suspect?"

"It won't be me. And you're not about to die from a gunshot wound...the gun is here just to keep you in line. You're going to die a natural death and I'm going to be someone who is extremely upset by your passing, because I'll be the last person to have seen you alive. As I was returning your dip and chip dish. I have to tell you, Miss Myrtle, I really hate that you've put me in this position. I like you. I thought perhaps I'd met my match." Maxine's mouth twisted. "This isn't my fault. It's yours."

"That's an interesting method of switching blame," said Myrtle with a short laugh. Her mouth was dry and her brain flew as she considered her options. "Did you do that for Naomi's death and Rose's? How convenient for you. To murder and yet remain blameless."

Maxine raised her carefully groomed eyebrows. "A little venom in your voice there, Miss M. But to answer your question...yes, I do blame them. These women weren't lambs to the slaughter, you know. Naomi Pelter was elbowing me out of any relationship I embarked on. If it weren't for her, I'd be married by now. I wouldn't be slogging through a boring day job and figuring out a household budget every quarter...I'd be doing what I wanted to do. And Naomi was a serial boyfriend-thief. She didn't care a thing for any of the men in question. Her goal was simply to end my relationships."

"It was a horrible way to die, though," said Myrtle reprovingly. "You can't think she deserved that."

"No," said Maxine thoughtfully. "No, I suppose she didn't deserve it. But the garden club speaker didn't do a very good job describing what the *effects* of eating Destroying Angel were."

Myrtle said, "Well, clearly, the speaker stated it was a fatal effect."

"Sure. But not that it was this drawn-out affair. I thought that perhaps Naomi would eat the mushrooms at the luncheon, go home, and be dead by the next day." Maxine shrugged.

"Was it difficult to obtain the mushrooms and put them on her salad?"

"Are you joking? It was a piece of cake, Miss Myrtle. Our town is virtually covered with Destroying Angel mushrooms. And the menu for the annual garden club luncheon is always the same and sitting out on the tables when we walk in."

Myrtle said, "What if they'd changed the menu for the luncheon this year? What would you have done then?"

"I did check online to ensure that the garden club president hadn't had a burst of culinary creativity and changed up the menu. But she hadn't. As usual, spinach salad with bacon bits, sliced hardboiled eggs, red onions...and button mushrooms. As the garden club speaker warned us, Destroying Angel mushrooms look just like button mushrooms. It's uncanny. While everyone was gabbing with each other, I added mushrooms to Naomi's plate. I took a few of the button mushrooms away, since Naomi seemed to have too many mushrooms. It worked perfectly."

"And Rose?" asked Myrtle. "How on earth did Rose deserve her fate? Hit over the head with a fire poker? What a horrid way to die."

Maxine tilted her head and her raven-black hair swept to the side. "Horrid? No, I don't think so. Instantaneous. There was no fear, Miss Myrtle. She didn't know what hit her."

"There *must* have been some type of anxiety though. After all, Rose clearly knew it was you. She'd seen you switching place cards, hadn't she? She knew that you and Naomi weren't exactly the best of friends. When Naomi died, she must have realized that you'd poisoned her. Did she threaten to expose you if you didn't pay her to keep quiet?" Myrtle gripped the knife tightly. Could she catch Maxine off-balance and make her drop that gun?

Maxine gave a wolfish grin. "Well, she didn't exactly put it that way. Rose was too refined, you know. She couldn't even blackmail like a normal crook. She said something along the lines of needing her retirement income supplemented. And if I could accommodate her by supplementing it, then there were certain things she might be persuaded to overlook."

"Didn't sound appealing?" Myrtle asked.

"Not particularly. Being blackmailed would mean that I was a victim, you see. I'm no victim. And who knows how long I'd be on the hook paying out? I don't have much money, myself. That's one of the reasons Naomi made me so furious. She was keeping me from finding a husband to help keep me afloat. I was tired of the day-to-day scrabble for money. And I certainly didn't have enough of it to share with Rose Mayfield." Maxine snorted at the idea.

"You tried to come after me the other night," said Myrtle reproachfully.

Maxine sighed. "As I've already mentioned, Miss Myrtle, I do not want to have to do this. I really like you. The only part of you I don't like is your nosy side. I knew you were starting to figure things out. I'd gone too far to get caught and spend the rest of my life in prison. You just kept *pushing*. And, really, if you're going to investigate crimes, you need to work on your poker face. I could clearly see that you were getting too close."

"You couldn't get in, though," said Myrtle a bit smugly.

"I thought *surely* you were one of those old ladies that slept with a window open or a door unlocked. I mean, really. You've lived in Bradley your entire, long life. Most of the people in this sleepy little village think it's the safest hamlet in the whole world." Maxine's brows drew together in consternation.

"But, you see, my son is the police chief. And so I get a sense of what's really going on in Bradley. It's a very safe place. But it's not safe enough to leave a window open. No place is."

Maxine gave a sudden laugh. "Were you chasing me with pepper spray, Miss M? Because that's what it looked like."

"Absolutely. I have a seer who advises me," said Myrtle haughtily.

Maxine laughed again and Myrtle, never one to take kindly at being laughed at, took the opportunity to lunge forward, extend the knife and slash at Maxine's hand that held the gun. Maxine's reflexes were too quick for her, though, and she batted the knife from Myrtle's hand with the gun. The knife clattered to the hardwood floor.

"That's enough," hissed Maxine. "Now move into the bedroom. You're about to die tragically in your sleep."

Myrtle snorted. "Shows what you know. My son will never buy that, Maxine."

"What do you mean?" grated Maxine.

"My son knows I never sleep. Ever. That will raise all kinds of red flags. And he is, after all, the police chief. If you smother me with a pillow, which is apparently what you're planning on doing, he's going to know."

"You have to die sometime. Why not in your own bed? I think he'll be more willing to buy that than you think. Get moving," said Maxine, shoving the gun into Myrtle's ribs.

The doorbell rang. Maxine and Myrtle both froze.

Chapter Nineteen

"Ignore it!" growled Maxine in a whisper.

But Myrtle cut off whatever else Maxine was planning on saying by taking her cane and hitting it as hard as she could on Maxine's forearm. Maxine howled in fury as the gun hit the floor. As she reached for it, Myrtle bolted for the front door, yanking it open.

Myrtle towered over the very startled looking mustachioed older man on her front step. He wore a green golf shirt with a "Greener Pastures Retirement Home" logo embroidered on it. "Mrs. Clover?" The man gaped at the wild-looking old woman in front of him.

Maxine let out a furious, guttural cry behind them and Myrtle shoved her way past the small man, thumping with her cane as she headed as fast as she could for the Greener Pastures van that was outside her home.

A grating voice shouldered its way into her brain. "The key is in the van."

She headed straight for the driver's seat.

Myrtle climbed in, tossing the cane into the passenger seat. The van was left running and the keys were, as promised by

Wanda, left in the ignition. Myrtle hit the lock on the door right as Maxine stumbled out onto Myrtle's front step, frightening the Greener Pastures man even further, if that were possible.

"What in the dickens are you doing?" barked a ferocious voice behind her in the van.

Myrtle swung around to see a cadaverous old woman with a huge, beak-like nose.

"Are you quite demented?" demanded the woman.

"Put your seatbelt on," she ordered as she pushed on the accelerator with her foot.

"You are demented!" gasped the old woman.

"Yes I am!" hollered Myrtle. "And if you don't shut your trap and put your seatbelt on, you're going to be sorry!"

Myrtle pushed hard on the accelerator again and the van's engine revved loudly.

"Take it out of park!" screeched the old woman.

Myrtle grasped the gearshift, put the van in reverse, and took off backward. The old woman's head bobbed violently. But she did put her seatbelt on.

Myrtle sped away down the street, heading for downtown Bradley.

"Where are we going?" asked the old woman peevishly. "I was supposed to be going on a tour of Greener Pastures."

"Quiet!" said Myrtle sharply. "Aside from one, short, slow drive earlier this afternoon, I haven't driven a vehicle for months. I need to focus."

She peered into her rearview mirror and spotted Maxine's car behind her, pulling out of her driveway and quickly moving toward the van. "She's lost her mind," muttered Myrtle.

"Must be catching!" carped her passenger.

Myrtle pressed harder on the accelerator and saw Maxine speed up in response.

"It's Mr. Toad's wild ride!" croaked the woman from the back.

But now Myrtle knew where she was heading. The square downtown—and the police station. And Red.

The dogwood-lined streets went by like a blur and Myrtle quickly reached the square downtown with its Revolutionary War soldier statue in the middle. And she saw that Red was just stepping out of the police station, sandwich in his hand, about to take a bite.

"A cop!" gasped the woman behind her and commenced to frantically beating on the van's window.

Myrtle laid on the horn and Red dropped his sandwich on the ground as he took in the sight of the Greener Pastures Retirement Home van being piloted by his mother—her white hair standing completely on end—with a frantic hostage slamming her fists against the back window.

Myrtle lowered the passenger side window and yelled, "Red! Maxine is the killer! She's behind me! With a gun!"

She hazarded another glance in the rearview mirror and saw Maxine catch sight of Red. Myrtle put the brake on, stopping the van in its tracks and blocking Maxine's way. Maxine slammed on her brakes, and then tried to throw the car into reverse...but was blocked by Erma Sherman's tank-like sedan, innocently coming up behind her. Erma had apparently felt she'd sobered up enough to be driving.

Maxine opened up her door and lunged out of her car, clearly planning to make a run for it. But Red was too fast for her. She'd only run a few steps in those heels of hers before Red caught up with her and grabbed her arms, jerking them behind her to put handcuffs on. Maxine jerked away and tried to run off, arms clasped behind her, but Red clutched her arm and yanked Maxine back, propelling her forward toward the police station.

"I've got a holding cell with your name on it," said Red grimly to Maxine. "And then I think it's time that I caught up with my mother a little. Mama, if you'll wait inside the station for me?"

"Let me just park the van first," said Myrtle, heading toward the vehicle. She saw Erma Sherman gaping in wonder at the scene playing out in front of her. The whole of Bradley would be hearing about this in the next few minutes. And whoever would have thought that Greener Pastures would prove to be Myrtle's salvation?

The old woman squawked as she spotted Myrtle moving toward the van.

"That's enough driving for today, Mama," said Red in a firm voice. "I'll move the van myself as soon as I put Ms. Tristan in a cell and put in a call to the state police. I guess I owe Greener Pastures a call, too." He groaned as he pushed the still-resisting Maxine into the station. Red called out politely to the old woman in the van, "Ma'am? You're welcome to come inside the station too while I sort all this out."

The old woman said peevishly, "But you're arresting the wrong person! The kidnapper was that wild looking woman there. With the crazy hair. She's the one who stole the van."

"She's no kidnapper," said Red with a long-suffering sigh. "She's my mother."

As Red disappeared into the back of the tiny police station to the even tinier cell with Maxine, Myrtle followed a bit further behind. She spotted her editor, Sloan Jones, gawking at her from the door of the *Bradley Bugle*. Myrtle put her nose in the air and sailed past, walking directly into the police station and sitting down on the old vinyl sofa. She bet Sloan was sorry now for shutting her down. Serves him right.

The state police had arrived, Maxine had been transported, still spitting mad, from the tiny holding cell to a different facility. The old man had walked downtown to collect the Greener Pastures van and the old woman passenger had left, still shooting Myrtle looks like daggers as she went.

Red sat down across from her in the cramped station. "Okay, Mama," he said in a weary voice. "I think I've managed to get all potential charges against you dropped. I do believe I finally convinced Mrs. Gladwell that you might, in fact, have saved her life by removing her from the vicinity of the gun-toting, vengeful Maxine."

"Silly old bat," muttered Myrtle. "Couldn't see that I was the heroine in all of this."

"She doesn't appear to be silly at all. She was sharp enough to be considering all manners of charges against you, including kidnapping and reckless abandon."

Myrtle furrowed her brow in concentration. "Reckless abandon? Is that even a crime? It sounds made-up to me."

"I believe she made it up, but she stated that her son is a lawyer. He sounded, frankly, like one of those ambulance-chasing types. Let's just hope she stays calmed down. I plan to bring Mrs. Gladwell a bouquet of flowers and a box of candy to try and make up with her. And to plead with her to ignore what happened." Red rubbed his face with a big hand.

"Bring her a bottle of Tanqueray and you'll probably be her best friend forever," said Myrtle with a sniff. "I can tell a heavy drinker when I see one."

"Can you? Can you tell that *I'm* about to become a heavy drinker with all the suffering you're putting me through?" growled Red.

"Me? None of this would have happened if you hadn't orchestrated an unwanted tour of Greener Pastures for me." Myrtle gave Red her most severe, chastising look. "Besides, as you mentioned, I saved Mrs. Gladwell's life, practically."

"The poor woman was merely in the wrong place at the wrong time," said Red. He reached over to his desk and took a swig from his coffee. He made a face. "That's been sitting there long enough to turn into sludge." He stared thoughtfully at Myrtle. "All right. We should stop fussing. I guess all's well that ends well."

But it hadn't quite ended. It seemed as though it had because Red drove her back home and sternly told her to put her feet up and rest. But an hour later, the doorbell rang. Myrtle felt a tickling sense of déjà vu as she slowly headed from her bedroom to the front door. Pasha had hissed and slunk off. Myrtle peered through the side window. The only difference this time was that when she saw the visitor was her editor, she didn't stop by the kitchen to get a knife before opening the door.

Sloan Jones stood there a little pink in the face. The corners of his mouth jerked upwards in a smile as Myrtle opened the door. "Mrs. Clover," he said hastily. "Red told me all about your adventure today. And that you'd solved the murders." Beads of perspiration appeared on his ever-expanding forehead. "Can I...may I come in?" He looked uncertainly at her.

Myrtle pursed her lips. "So, suddenly, I'm a good person to talk to. I suppose you're wanting to interview me and write up the whole story yourself and put out a special edition of the paper? The answer is no." Myrtle started to close the door.

Sloan quickly stammered out, "No! No, Mrs. Clover, that's actually not what I want. I want you to write the story yourself. A whole, huge feature. I told Red just as much...that I *had* to get your story and that you were the best...the *only* person for the job. I'm in your corner, Mrs. Clover."

Myrtle relaxed a bit. "Well. That's nice to hear. I'll take you up on that, Sloan. I'll email your story in the next couple of hours." She paused, noticing for the first time that he held something in his hands. "What's this?"

Sloan looked down in surprise at the dish, as if he'd forgotten about its presence, himself. "Oh. Yes. This is just a little something I whipped up at home. Sort of an I'm-so-sorry gift." He grimaced. "It's better than it sounds. I haven't been a lifelong bachelor for nothing...I promise I can cook."

"It sounds delightful, Sloan," Myrtle said graciously, beaming at him. She was in much better humor now that her place as an investigative reporter had been re-established. "What is it?"

"It's my specialty. A mushroom and rice casserole," said Sloan with a happy smile.

Myrtle put the casserole into the fridge after ascertaining that Sloan did *not* pick his own mushrooms, but purchased them from the Bradley farmer's market. She was just about to sit down at the desk to type up her riveting story for the paper when the doorbell rang once again. This time she was glad to see who was at the door.

Miles, looking quite sober and not at all hung over, walked in and sat down on the sofa. "I want to hear all about it," he said, "every last word." He was carrying a bottle of wine, two glasses and a corkscrew.

"I'm writing it up for the paper, you know," said Myrtle with a playful look at him. "And haven't you had enough to drink today?"

"Like I'm going to wait for the newspaper to find out how this ends," said Miles grimly. "And...yes, I had had enough to drink...until I heard about this. So go ahead...spill it."

As Myrtle told him the story his eyes grew wider and wider until he resembled an owl.

At the end, they sat in silence, thinking it through and taking small sips of their wine. "The funny thing is," said Myrtle slowly, "is that I still rather like Maxine. I know she tried to kill me and everything, but I believe she genuinely thought she had no other option."

"I suppose she'll have a lot of free time now. Might come up with some better ways she could have handled the situation instead of resorting to murder," said Miles.

Myrtle smiled. Miles always sounded a bit prim when he was being self-righteous.

The phone rang and they both jumped a little. "No one will leave me alone," grumbled Myrtle, picking up the phone. "Hello?" she belligerently demanded.

She listened for a moment and then started smiling. Fumbling with the phone for a moment, she managed to put it on speaker.

A voice on the other end was droning, "...so, in light of the recent events, Mrs. Clover, and the complaints lodged by Mrs. Gladwell, we have no choice but to remove your name, at least temporarily, from the Greener Pastures retirement home waiting list."

Myrtle winked at Miles and he raised his glass in a toast.

About the Author:

Elizabeth writes the Southern Quilting mysteries and Memphis Barbeque mysteries for Penguin Random House and the Myrtle Clover series for Midnight Ink and independently. She blogs at ElizabethSpannCraig.com/blog, named by Writer's Digest as one of the 101 Best Websites for Writers. Elizabeth makes her home in Matthews, North Carolina, with her husband. She's the mother of two.

Sign up for Elizabeth's free newsletter to stay updated on releases:

https://elizabethspanncraig.com/newsletter/

This and That

I love hearing from my readers. You can find me on Facebook as Elizabeth Spann Craig Author, on Twitter as elizabethscraig, on my website at elizabethspanncraig.com, and by email at elizabethspanncraig@gmail.com.

Thanks so much for reading my book...I appreciate it. If you enjoyed the story, would you please leave a short review on the site where you purchased it? Just a few words would be great. Not only do I feel encouraged reading them, but they also help other readers discover my books. Thank you!

Did you know my books are available in print and ebook formats? And most of the Myrtle Clover series is available in audio. Find them on Audible or iTunes.

Interested in having a character named after you? In a preview of my books before they're released? Or even just your name listed in the acknowledgments of a future book? Visit my Patreon page at https://www.patreon.com/elizabethspanncraig
.

I have Myrtle Clover tote bags, charms, magnets, and other goodies at my Café Press shop: https://www.cafepress.com/cozymystery

If you'd like an autographed book for yourself or a friend, please visit my Etsy page.

I'd also like to thank some folks who helped me put this book together. Thanks to my cover designer, Karri Klawiter, for her awesome covers. Thanks to my editor, Judy Beatty, for all of her help. Thanks to beta readers Amanda Arrieta and Dan Harris for all of their helpful suggestions and careful reading. Thanks, as always, to my family and readers.

Other Works by the Author:

Myrtle Clover Series in Order (be sure to look for the Myrtle series in audio, ebook, and print):

Pretty is as Pretty Dies

Progressive Dinner Deadly

A Dyeing Shame

A Body in the Backyard

Death at a Drop-In

A Body at Book Club

Death Pays a Visit

A Body at Bunco

Murder on Opening Night

Cruising for Murder

Cooking is Murder

A Body in the Trunk

Cleaning is Murder

Edit to Death

Hushed Up (late 2019)

Southern Quilting Mysteries in Order:

Quilt or Innocence

Knot What it Seams

Quilt Trip
Shear Trouble
Tying the Knot
Patch of Trouble
Fall to Pieces
Rest in Pieces
On Pins and Needles
Fit to be Tied

The Village Library Mysteries in Order (Debuting 2019):

Checked Out
Overdue (late 2019)

Memphis Barbeque Mysteries in Order (Written as Riley Adams):

Delicious and Suspicious
Finger Lickin' Dead
Hickory Smoked Homicide
Rubbed Out

And a standalone "cozy zombie" novel: Race to Refuge, written as Liz Craig

Made in the USA
Columbia, SC
06 March 2023

13421347R00111